THE CAVERN OF AHTŪN

RIMROCK

written and illustrated by
Peter Sandel

THE CAVERN OF AHTŪN

RIMROCK

written and illustrated by
PETER SANDEL

ISBN: 979-8-9855192-2-8 (e-book)

ISBN: 979-8-9855192-3-5 (paperback)

THE RIMROCK CANYON

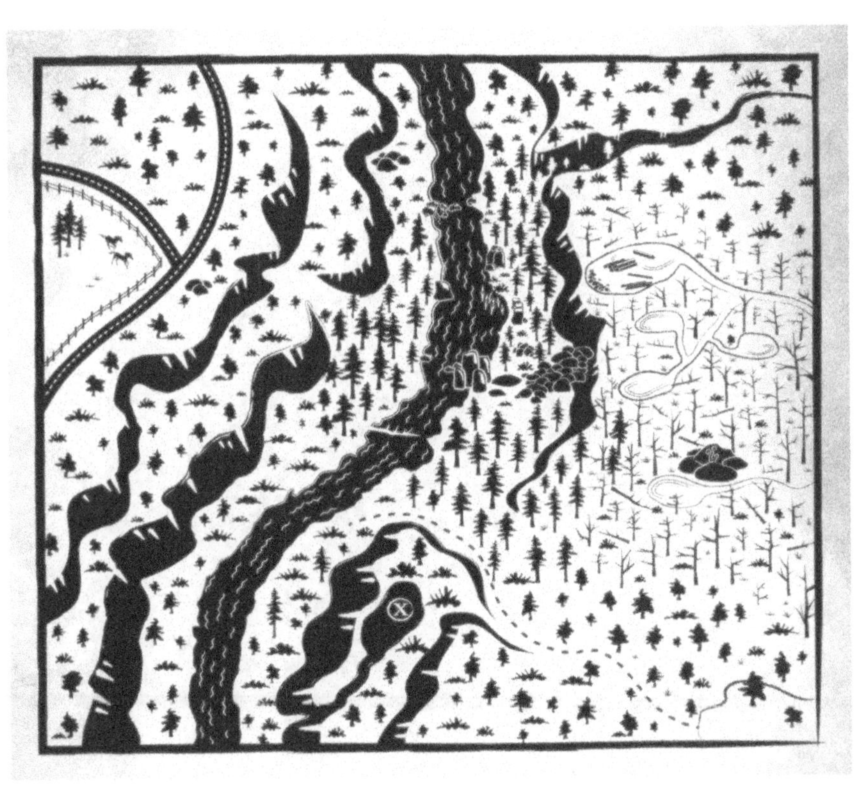

AUTHOR'S NOTE

In this second book of the trilogy, The Cavern of Ahtūn, Teek, Kanti, Cicci, Peeps, and Digger realize that that the stolen illumination stone and the arrival of the rats were merely the signs of a much greater concern looming ahead, the destruction of their habitat by humans.

Who are *you* on the inside? You may find out as you read the Rimrock Trilogy.

I hope you enjoy book 2.

– Peter

1

AN UNEXPECTED VISITOR

Ravens never miss a thing, particularly this raven. Kanti peered down over the sheer columns of the rimrock, listening to the distant roar of the river and quiet rush of the wind, mixed with the occasional call of a songbird.

From his position soaring high above, the shimmering rapids, the long pools were little more than a narrow silvery ribbon, meandering its way to the hazy north. Gusts of cool fresh air swept up the canyon and buffeted the glistening black feathers of his wings. He hung suspended, cocking his head this way and that, and scanned the bank below.

The early spring breeze brought with it the sweet and savory scent of fresh yellow sage blooms. He floated above the cliffs like a kite, letting the sunlight of the young day warm the black feathers on his back. The few remaining white patches of snow reminded him of the long tough winter. Fresh new shoots of grasses and early flowers signaled the beginning of abundant renewal, a promising new season of bounty and comfort.

The early morning was his favorite part of the day for surveying and assessing all the bustling activity and goings-on. He carefully observed and recorded in his mind the whereabouts of caches from the fishing, foraging, and hunting—paying close attention to what everyone was collecting, hiding, and storing. At dawn, the creatures of the canyon were already busy. They were the most active, after the thaw of a long, frozen winter. A a high priority—well one of them anyway—was to fill their bellies. Calories were the currency.

Gliding over the edge of his range, Kanti felt an overpowering need to know what was going on below. But all this activity was not the reason for his flight nor the reason for his destination. This morning he was on his way to visit a friend at a familiar bend in the river, at secret location known to a very few. His destination could only be seen from above, if one knew just where to look that is. He had news to report and an important request to make.

Kanti was experienced at flying through the canyon and knew that soaring over to one side, just above the rimrock would give him the updraft he needed to keep him aloft with less effort. Soaring is one thing and landing is another. This descent would be different than the maneuvers he was used to. Glancing down to the river below, he noticed quick movements.

Ah! Fisk. He is chasing fish, he thought to himself.

He circled as Fisk, the otter, darted and zig-zagged across a steamy deep pool, just below some rapids. From Kanti's vantage point directly overhead, Fisk was easy to follow. Silvery flashes from a school of trout could be seen just in front of his nose. The fish were never a match for Fisk's ability to slip through the water. With one quick twist and turn, the agile otter caught his breakfast.

That, thought Kanti, *looks like a lot of work. It suits Fisk though. Too bad he eats them the moment he catches them, I would not mind tasting some of that if he could just think to stuff one in the bunchgrass on the riverbank one time. He is a good fellow, that Fisk; maybe I will mention something to him.*

Kanti's attention returned to his mission and his destination. Tipping his wings, he pointed himself purposefully toward a very special place—a distinct bend in the river. A place where, over the eons, the cliffs had split apart. He began to plan his landing. There would be little room for gliding, and he'd have to drop straight down or risk possibly bouncing off one of the surrounding walls of the basalt rock face. Kanti had never actually been inside the village of Rimrock before and was a bit apprehensive. He hoped his landing would be successful.

For the squirrels of Rimrock, this happened to be the first morning after a very long winter hibernation. Still groggy from his slumber, Teek shuffled down his hallway to respond to an urgent rapping on his front door. He opened it to the bright light reflecting off patches of snow still clinging to the shadier areas around the tiny village. The brightness of the early day lit the inside of his burrow, glancing off the shards of mirror and brightly lighting Teek's face, making him squint and blink. The figure at the door was backlit and in the bright light, Teek could only make out the outline of his neighbor, a squirrel named Timit. Timit's head turned quickly, glancing nervously behind him, then back at Teek.

"Teek! Teek!" was his urgent greeting.

"Yes, yes, good morning. What brings you over at this hour?" Teek managed to mutter.

"I am sorry to have awakened you," Timit replied.

"Oh well, you did not really awaken me, I am just getting a bit of a slower start today," Teek mumbled as he turned.

Cicci poked her head out into the hallway.

"Who is it, Teek?" Cicci had risen just before Teek, to rummage through their larder to start the day with a nibble of something.

"It is Timit," came his labored reply. "Would you like to come in, Timit? It is a bit chilly."

"Oh, no, thank you though. I came to tell you that there is a large black bird that has landed in the central grassy area, in the middle of the village, there, on the other side of Rimrock creek." He pointed with his paw hurriedly out past the creek.

"He asked for you by name. He appears to know you."

Teek peered across the way toward the central grassy area. Steam rose from the little meandering stream, misting the large dark looming figure. Lit from above, it appeared to Teek as simply a black shadowy shape, large and imposing, quite a specter to behold.

Trying to figure out who the visitor might be, Teek leaned to peer around Timit, blinking into the sparkling brightness of the morning.

Once he realized who it was, he snapped to alertness, and sharply blurted, "I will be right out, thank you Timit!" Timit turned and scampered back to his home and stood behind the protection of his front door.

"Kanti? Is that you?" Teek crossed the village and scrambled briskly over the rock slab bridge, and onto the grass, to peer up at his dear old friend.

"Quiulup! It is I, my little friend. I must say, it is good to see you. You look well. How was your hibernation? I have missed you and Cicci?"

"Cicci will be so glad to see you. I am pleased that you have come to visit, and I... well, we that is, have missed you."

By this time, many villagers were peering out of their doorways to witness the large, imposing, and unexpected visitor standing in the middle of their village. Seek, the story elder, emerged from the double doors of Colony Hall.

Formerly called "The Great Hall," it was renamed shortly after the return of the Illumination Stone, in honor and recognition of its importance to the entire colony. The hall once again served as the gathering place for historical stories during the special positioning of the bright light of day and the cool light of night. The Illumination Stone would once again illuminate the Story Elder. Seek approached slowly and cautiously toward them, glancing at villagers peering from their doorways. He was torn between his sense of responsibility to the colony and to the intimidating and seemingly threatening presence of the large black bird.

Seek finally overcame his instinctive fear enough to approach, and so, he began his greeting. "To what do we owe the honor of your visit sir?"

Cicci then appeared on the grassy area, interrupting the beginning of Seek's greeting.

"Kanti!" She scurried up to greet him. "Kanti! We have missed you so. It has been a long winter. How have you been doing?"

She positioned herself directly in front of him, her admiration was difficult for her to put into words. And so, she stood, nervously wringing her paws, gazing up at him.

"Well, well, Cicci, good to see you again. There is no time to tell you all about everything that is going on. For now, I need to share some news from down-river."

Seek, politely acknowledged Kanti's reunion with Cicci, and then began speaking again.

"Is this a friend of yours Teek, or should we be ditching for our very lives?" He made this comment with a chuckle and in his most charming manner, as leader of the colony.

Teek introduced Seek to Kanti. "Kanti, I would like you to meet Seek. He is our Story Elder. As you know, because of your help, Kanti, we have the Illumination Stone back in place in Colony Hall and we are once again gathering together and listening to historical stories."

"So, *you* are Kanti," interjected Seek. "I have heard many wonderful things about you. I have wanted so much to thank you."

"The canyon is a concern for all of us," Kanti replied, adding, "Where, may I ask, is Eechius, your other story elder?"

Teek now lowered his head and gazed with a faraway look into the grass at his feet. Seek answered quickly.

"I am afraid Eechius has passed."

Kanti was silent and thoughtful for a moment. He knew that Eechius meant a lot to Teek. "I am sorry for this great loss." Then he turned and spoke directly to Teek. "You are so fortunate for having known him. You carry his wisdom with you."

RETURN OF THE HUMANS

Down river, a sudden loud roar awakened the encampment of the rats. The humans had returned to the landing, resuming the work on the subdivision overlooking the canyon. The giant yellow monsters began to move, blowing dark smoke and growling to life. The rats heard the sounds and felt the vibration. Steam began to roll out of the pipes as they scrambled around in panic. Over the winter they had piled up rocks, sticks, and dead branches, plugging up the ends of the black tubes. They had crowded themselves inside, massing together for warmth. Writhing, wriggling, clawing, and biting, they had spent the bitter cold winter nesting in dead grass, pine needles, and their own excrement. Only the stronger rats survived the long, cold winter. The older, or injured rats were killed, and lay dead. Others had been eaten. Their bones were stuffed into the dead branches, stones, and piled-up dirt that blocked the ends of the pipes. As the pipes were lifted and moved out of the way, the debris and rats all fell out of either end. The workers were surprised and alarmed. They began shouting and backing away. The pipe at the bottom of the pile, held the alpha rat, Sleg. Attendant rats awakened him with screeches and scratches to alert him to the noise and the threat. A less experienced rat attempted to rouse him from his slumber. This rat received a fatal bite to the neck.

Early spring had left a few drifts of snow clinging to the rocks, around the edges of the brush, and the trunks of the junipers, but the humans seemed anxious to start construction as soon as possible, in anticipation of the warmer months ahead. As the jaws of the mechanical monsters began to grip and lift the pipes, out poured the rats and the debris.

This horrified the human workers, who began shouting in surprise and alarm, climbing up onto their large yellow monsters to escape the chaotic exodus.

"How in the devil? Where did they come from?" one exclaimed.

The explosion of rats was as offensive for the humans to smell as it was to witness. One human drew a pistol and began firing into the scurrying and scattering mass. He managed to kill a couple and injure a few more. The rest of the rats instantly changed directions in unison, stampeding over the edge of the embankment. Another human finished off the rats that had been shot and wounded with the blade of his shovel.

"Next time," one human exclaimed, catching his breath, "we pack everything out with us and pile it in the warehouse. Get on the radio and call Dennis. Ask him to bring a truck out here... Have you ever seen anything like this?"

"I have not!" an older human more senior member of the team in an orange hardhat replied. "Are those the same rats that live in cities? How did they get out here? Some of them are enormous!"

"To the bush, to the bush!" screeched Sleg, now waddling and rolling down the hill.

The hoard of marauding rats swarmed into the thick bitter brush, just off the landing. Sleg and his attendant rats found an opening in the boulders to squeeze into, leaving the rest of the rats, including females and offspring, to fend for themselves.

"Bring Eek to me!" he ordered.

Eek was already crouched nearby. He approached Sleg.

"It appears that our time at this encampment is at an end, Eek. We will find this Rimrock, and we take it for our own! Now go!" he screamed.

Without a word, Eek scurried away. Sleg turned to his attendant rats and screamed again. "Well, do not just sit there! Start digging out under these rocks! I need a place to stay while we search for Rimrock!"

Eek turned to his band of underlings, screeching "We must find Rimrock... now!"

Kanti and Apitah, the muha (red-tailed hawk), had both witnessed the entire event. Kanti, because he had shown up to find out what the humans were doing, and Apitah just happened to soar overhead when it occurred.

3

NEWS FROM KANTI

Kanti stood before the silent squirrels on the grassy area in the middle of the village. They waited for his words. He then reported what he had witnessed two cycles before. In a low, resolute tone, he spoke.

"They are back."

"Who is back?" Teek stopped and turned his face from Seek, back toward Kanti.

"The humans. They have returned to the place downriver where the rats were living. I watched them. This time they have come back to dig up our homes."

"You saw this?" asked Teek.

"I did. Then Apitah... do you remember the muha that killed Ish the snake?"

"I will never forget."

"Well, Apitah was soaring overhead, and he witnessed the same thing. The humans are taking the pipes away. I fear for Rimrock more than ever now. Something has happened. This time it is different. There is someone named Dennis Digwood. We heard his name over and over. He is the one that leads the humans. There is something different about him. He shouted at everyone as though he needed to do something quickly. Once they picked up the pipes and killed some rats, he left in a hurry. Apitah and I followed him. We think we know where he lives."

"Where are the rats?" asked Teek.

"I do not know. No one knows," replied Kanti. "The humans came with their monsters that roar and blow smoke. The rats scattered. The humans killed some of them. There is something else. I am not sure but, well, this Dennis Digwood, he seemed to be aware."

"Aware?"

"Somehow he seemed different from the other humans."

"How?"

"Teek, I think he understands what we are saying. I think he understands the language of animals."

"How could this be?"

"I do not know yet, but I intend to find out."

Cicci had been talking to other squirrels and so did not hear the exchange. She had been waiting as patiently as she could for the chance to speak to Kanti. Now she could wait no longer. "So, what is happening Kanti? Do you need Teek's help?" Then she remembered that he was a guest in their village. Although Rimrock was isolated and received few visitors, it was still customary to offer hospitality to friendly visitors in need.

"I apologize, all that can wait. Kanti, are you thirsty? Are you hungry?" Cicci asked.

"Thank you, Cicci, but I drank some water before I set out to meet you."

"I should tell you, my dear Kanti," she went on, "that we now have another drink to offer you—pine-nut brew!"

"Do you now?" Kanti replied. "Perhaps, before I leave, I would accept a sip. That would be very nice before I continue on my way."

Cicci turned and nodded to some young squirrels who ran errands for the leaders in the village. She turned back to Kanti. "I shall never forget Apitah. He is well?"

"He is more than well. He has become highly regarded. His bravery and power have become legend. He is now a leader among the muhas." Kanti continued. "Apitah is not the only hero, though. There is another highly regarded creature in this canyon."

"Who?" asked Teek.

"You," replied Kanti. "That is why I am here."

"Me?" asked Teek, with astonishment.

"Yes," Kanti replied. "You see, Teek, you and your band of ground squirrels not only found the Illumination Stone and returned it to Rimrock, but you also encountered many creatures in this canyon. Some of them have wings, some swim, and some crawl or scamper. But they all have the same concern—a place to live. And that, my dear Teek, is why it is important that you journey out again. The creatures in this canyon are stronger together. And they need you."

"But Kanti... how can I possibly figure out how to help everyone in the canyon? I am just a squirrel."

Cicci reached out and put one of her paws on Teek's shoulder and said, "Kanti, surely our journey to retrieve the Illumination Stone was never meant to... to do all that!"

Kanti replied, "Cicci, I think that something even more important than finding the Illumination Stone occurred. You, Teek, Peeps, and yes, even Cheeks... well, you changed things. I sense that there is a new energy that I have not felt before, and I feel that it is very powerful. I also feel that it may be just in time. We must not wait."

"What do you want me, um, I mean *us*, to do?" Teek asked with a confirming glance to Cicci.

"What do you think you *should* do, Teek?" Kanti asked.

Seek began to imagine where all this talk was headed, and he spoke up. "Look here, Kanti! Teek? You do remember that you are to assume Eechius' position as Story Elder, yes? Teek? Besides, I do not even know how long *I* will be around… you are critical to the future of this colony! You cannot continue to take these risks!"

"Seek," Teek replied, "if you recall, one of the big lessons that Cicci took away from our last adventure, was that outright exposure, and a connection with other creatures in our canyon actually makes all of us safer!"

"Well, yes, Teek, dear," Cicci added, "but that does not mean that it must always be you!"

"Yes, Cicci, for now it does," corrected Kanti. "It is Teek they have heard of. It is the biggest story of the canyon, from muha to mouse."

"Kanti, what do we do?" Teek asked again.

Kanti turned back to Teek. "I need you to meet me outside the walls of your colony. I will give you more information that must be kept away from the ears of innocent gossipers. I will be waiting for you just beyond the opening. You should leave before the bright light of day appears twice. Only bring those with you with whom you have the utmost trust—like Cicci here."

"Of course," replied Teek.

Cicci lowered her eyes to the ground, appreciating her recognition.

"Now I must fly," Kanti concluded, "Cicci, I will have to miss your kind offer of pine nut brew for now. Can we share a cup when you get to the Pine Stone Inn?"

The young errand squirrel was just now headed their way with a large bowl, unaware of the sudden change of plans.

"The Pine Stone Inn? Oh, that will be very nice! It will be good to see 'ol Wuchak again!" said Teek. "He is still there? Is he well?"

"He is still there, and he is well. Now, I must go." Kanti lifted his gaze toward the sky and spread his massive wings. "You might want to cover your faces. I can stir up a lot of dust sometimes."

With that, he leaped into the air, flapping his wings for vertical lift, creating such a rush of wind that snow particles and sand hissed through the air in all directions. As he ascended, he had to shove off the rock face with his feet halfway up to clear the rim of the cliff. Silhouetted by the bright light of day overhead, he disappeared over the edge out of sight. Teek looked upward, his dark eyes blinking against the light as his old friend sailed away.

"He sure does leave suddenly, doesn't he?" asked Seek.

Cicci turned to him and nodded.

Teek sat on the flat rock overlooking the river. It was the earlier part of the next day and still cool. A watery breeze sent ripples across the pool before him, and the sweet pungent fragrance of water plants filled his nose. A mother duck and her brood slid through the narrow channels between the cattails on the opposite shore. She had eight ducklings in her brood. They stayed as close to her as they could, some even rode on her back. No telling what monsters lurked below. She and her family were Common Merganser Ducks, a fish-eating duck, common in the Deschutes Canyon. She had taught them to stick close to shore.

Teek watched them pass quietly by. *Could there be a nicer spot anywhere else? It is no wonder the humans want to live here.* He thought.

His mind then returned to the seemingly unsolvable problem—the fate of the canyon.

So, Dennis Digwood understands what the creatures say. How could this human have been awakened? Well, if he can understand me, then he can be reasoned with. It is a bit of a journey, but, with Kanti's help, I could show up at his dwelling. Perhaps he will listen. The creatures in this canyon are not going to lose their homes, not if I have anything to say about it! he pondered.

"Teek?" Cicci had been looking for Teek. She knew this was his favorite rock, but he had never visited it alone. "What are you doing?"

"Nothing, just sitting here enjoying the river."

"Well, you had better be careful, a koos or any other predator could see you on that rock. You cannot just sit there alone and gaze into the river! What are you thinking about anyway? Tell me."

"Nothing much, just thinking about the canyon and the life we have here and how tragic it would be if our homes were destroyed to make way for those huge human dwellings. There must be something that can be done. Cicci, I need to go away for a cycle or so. Three lights of the day from now, I should be back."

"Oh no. Where are you going?"

"Not far, I just need to go see Dennis Digwood."

"Teek?"

"Now do not worry. I will be careful."

"Teek?"

"Kanti will accompany me."

"That is because this is a dangerous journey!"

"Cicci, everywhere is dangerous. Who better than me?"

"Hmm, let me see, anyone else?"

Teek sighed. "Not this time. I need to be the one to go."

"You sound set on this. When are you leaving?"

"Two cycles from now."

"When were you going to tell me?"

"I just now thought of it," Teek replied.

"Oh Teek, you will worry me to death, do you know that?"

"Come down off of that rock and come back to the village."

⁂

Two cycles later, Teek and Kanti traveled together. Teek scampered on the ground and Kanti flew from branch to branch.

Kanti called down to him. "Good thing this is not very far, traveling with you would become tiresome." He swooped down and landed in front of Teek, saying, "I am only coming with you because I know that you would have gone anyway, and this is too dangerous. You are lucky that I did not tell Cicci where you were going."

"I told her."

"She wonders, you know. I had to tell her that you had not told me!"

"Kanti, I told her."

"You did?"

"Yes."

Kanti thought for a moment, and then continued. "Teek, you cannot take this on yourself. I have watched this Digwood fellow. He is dangerous, he is only concerned with himself, and he is unpredictable. Most humans are dangerous and unpredictable, but this one... this one is... well, this one..."

"Yes, I know, Kanti. I will be careful."

"He is also clever. He will try to lure you in and capture you. No, this is not a good idea. By the way, what do you have in your satchel?"

"Squirrel food."

"May I see?"

"No. There is nothing to see."

"Teek, you know that I need to see what every creature hides, and where they have hidden it. You know I must look in your satchel. You know that I will not be able to go further unless I..."

"All right! Here, see? Squirrel food!"

"Yes, yes. I know, I know. It is just what I do."

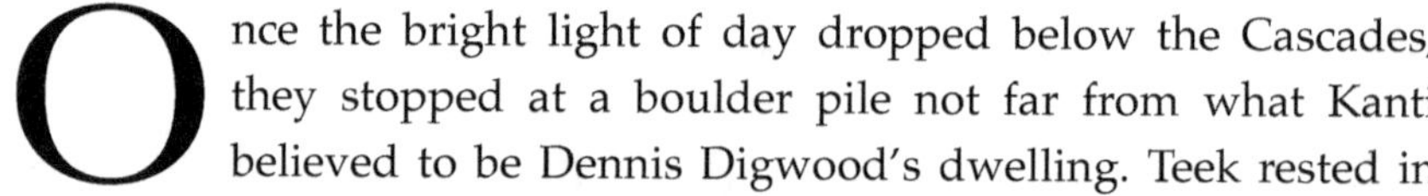

Once the bright light of day dropped below the Cascades, they stopped at a boulder pile not far from what Kanti believed to be Dennis Digwood's dwelling. Teek rested in the boulder pile while Kanti rested in the upper branches of a ponderosa, his favorite perch.

At first light, Kanti dropped down to the rock he thought Teek had crawled under and called to him. "Teek? Teek? Are you awake?"

"I am awake."

Teek poked his head out from underneath one of the other boulders. Kanti hopped over to him, from where he had mistakenly been calling.

"There you are. I must go grab something to eat. I will be back very soon. Do not go anywhere."

"I will be right here. I am not going anywhere without you."

Kanti returned much later than he had led Teek to believe. Ground squirrels, by nature, can be a little impatient. A raven, on the other hand, since it is interested in many things, is somewhat easily distracted. They notice everything and must investigate. When Kanti eventually made it back, the two set off for the last leg of the journey to Dennis Digwood's dwelling.

His home was spacious and imposing. There was a large, long black shining beast waiting right out in front. It did not move. Dennis had a separate home office where he did much of his "plotting." Kanti and Teek did not understand this of course, and so when Dennis and his investor emerged from the office, Kanti and Teek didn't see them, because they were facing in the other direction. Lucinda Musgrab, Dennis' investor, noticed the rodent and large raven on the walkway in front of them first and released a scream that would have startled a slug.

Kanti took off, flapping his large black wings for all he was worth until he reached the top of a nearby tree, and Teek ditched under a boulder so fast that in the blink of an eye, he was nowhere to be seen. They were, however, close enough to hear everything that Lucinda yelled once she stopped screaming.

"You don't even have your own property controlled; how do you expect me to have any level of confidence that the rest of your properties are free of vermin? If you don't get rid of them, I'm pulling my investment!" she said, quickly slipping on her soft black leather jacket, and looking at him with a piercing glare.

Dennis called after her. "I promise you they will all be gone before the first open house. They are as good as dead! The next time you are here, they will be nowhere to be seen."

With that, Lucinda Musgrab climbed into the long black beast, and it carried her away in a great hurry.

"Get out here now, so I can start by killing the both of you!"

Neither Teek nor Kanti budged while listening to Dennis rant and yell at the top of his lungs until Trisha, Dennis' wife, emerged from their front door.

"Who are you yelling and swearing at?"

"Nobody!"

"Come inside. You know, soon we will have neighbors. It would be very embarrassing if anyone hears that."

Once the door closed, Teek scampered as fast as he could off Dennis' property and into the forest. He didn't stop scampering until he reached the mound of boulders where he had spent the previous night.

Fwoop, fwoop, Kanti landed.

"That," Kanti said, "is a good example of why you never awaken most humans. So, what do you think now?"

Teek stared straight ahead in amazement. "I think that there is no getting through to that one. I just thought that we should give reasoning with him a chance. Now I know. We now know more than we did. He is driven by something else. I do not understand that female. She seems to consider me to be a rat! I'm no rat, and besides, I belong here. This is where I'm from!"

"She is from far away Teek. Where she comes from, there is no difference between you and a rat."

Teek stared at Kanti in disbelief. "There is as much difference as dry ground and water!"

"If we set out right now, we can make it back to Rimrock before darkness. It is easy for me, but can you make it fast enough?"

"The sooner, the better."

"We will talk about this again when the bright light of day is back in the sky. Once we return you to Rimrock, know that I will be back at first light," Kanti said.

Teek and Kanti parted ways at the entrance to the passage into the village of Rimrock.

From the back of the burrow, Cicci heard Teek come in. Poking her head into the hallway she called to him.

Cicci greeted Teek with a quick nuzzle. "You are home. Now I can stop worrying. How did it go?"

"Not well." Teek shuffled down the hallway slowly.

"Am I supposed to be surprised? Are you all right? Are you hungry?"

"I am fine... yes, I am hungry."

"Is Kanti all right? I am surprised he agreed to go."

"He did not want to, but he went to protect me. At least we know what we are dealing with now. This human cannot be reasoned with. He must be stopped. I am discussing this with Kanti again when the bright light returns to the sky."

4

CHANGING OF THE GUARDIANS

Two young humans, Sofia and Jake sat at the edge of the cliff overlooking the canyon, their legs dangling. The warm wind was stronger at the top of the cliff. They listened to the quiet breeze mixed with the distant roar of the river below. Sofia watched as Jake's long black hair waved and whipped around.

There is something very serene about his face, she thought.

His eyes were closed as if soaking in the waning afternoon with the sun sitting just above the now shadowy Cascades. The breeze was warmed by the late afternoon sun.

"What are you thinking about?" she asked him.

"Oh, not much," he replied.

He was a boy of few words; Sofia liked that; she had enough words for both of them.

"Okay then, here's another question: What are you?"

He looked at her, with puzzlement on his face, lifting one eyebrow.

"What do you mean, what am I?" he replied.

"You know, your heritage."

"Oh, I'm Nimiipuu."

"What poo?"

"Nimiipuu. It means 'The People'."

"Oh... what people? Are you some kind of Indian?"

"Have you ever heard of the Nez Perce?"

"Sure!"

"Well, that is what the French called us, and that name stuck, not surprisingly, even though it makes no sense to us because none of us ever pierced our noses."

Sofia had never heard her new friend speak so much. Usually, the shy boy limited his sentences to three or four words, and mostly only after being asked a direct question.

She thought, *wow, this subject really got him going.* "Nez Perce means you pierce your noses?"

"Well, yes but we really didn't. I mean some people might have, but it wasn't a thing."

"Oh."

They sat in silence. Then Sofia continued. "So, your name is Jake?"

"Jake is my English name, not my real name."

"I see. So, what is your real name?"

"Hmm, I'm not sure you could pronounce it," he chuckled.

He laughs! Sofia thought to herself. "Really? I'm pretty good at things like that. Let's try."

They sat again in silence as Sofia waited patiently, her gaze was fixed on his face. She knew that this was a very personal subject for Jake.

Jake leaned forward and peered over the edge. Seeming to make a difficult decision about this line of conversation, he began.

"Okay, first, we Nimiipuu only take one name. It is difficult for many people to pronounce because *our* names can have sounds that don't exist in the English language." He paused, then began again. "In my tribe, taking a traditional name is a way of honoring an ancestor."

"Well?... what is it?" she said with impatience in her voice.

His head turned sharply to face her. He had a stern look in his eyes.

"Sorry," she said. "Go ahead... please."

He stood up. Sofia's eyes followed his face. She thought, *oh boy, I've done it now, he's leaving.*

But Jake wasn't leaving. He took a deep breath and proudly spoke his name, as though he were proclaiming it to the entire canyon.

"My name is Ipsusnute! That is who I am!"

"What? Would you mind saying that again? I need to hear it one more time!"

"I told you it was diff…"

"Just say it one more time."

He stood for a moment, then said "It is pronounced Ip-sus-nute."

"Ipsusnute?"

"Yes."

"Your real name is Ipsusnute?"

"Yes."

"Wow, that *is*, sort of… different."

"Not to me it isn't," he replied indignantly.

Sofia opened her eyes wide as she responded with an idea. "What if I call you 'Ipsus' or 'Nute'? That way, I'm referring to your real name and being respectful, but it's a lot easier… sort of a nickname."

"Sure." Then, another long pause as he thought. "I sorta like Nute."

"Nute it is!"

Nute smiled. He seemed to open up and feel more comfortable. Sofia liked the new boldness showing through. She was getting to know him.

"Watch this," he said, as he picked up a pinecone. "Do you see that flat rock down there?"

"Nute, there are rocks everywhere. Which one?"

"That lighter one, down the hill, straight ahead. I can throw this pinecone and hit the top of that rock!"

"No, that's too far, it must be… well I don't know… quite a distance away…"

Nute threw the pinecone with surprising force and accuracy. As he claimed, it hit the top of the rock.

Sofia's face turned to look at Nute. She was astonished. "Wow, did you get lucky, or can you do that again?"

"Every time," he said with pride. "I was raised throwing pinecones with other kids. We'd throw pinecones to see who could throw it farthest and be the most accurate."

Nute threw another pinecone and hit the top of the rock again, almost in the same spot.

"Amazing!" Sofia kept staring at the targeted rock. "That has to be good for something, Nute."

"Yeah, wasting time."

"You mustn't think that. You never know how something can come back to you."

Nute didn't realize it at the time, but his ability to throw pinecones accurately from a distance would eventually prove to be quite valuable.

Sofia scanned the canyon, then looked back at Nute. "Let's head down now."

Sofia hopped up suddenly, the same way she used to do with her grandfather, Walter. She stepped with lively and confident agility down the trail toward the river, way below. Nute followed, without all the hopping.

5

DIGGER'S DISCOVERY

"Well," muttered Teek. "We have much to do. Cicci, I will go back to Stonewood Place and pack our satchels for the journey. Can you go see if Peeps is interested in joining us?"

"He should be home with his momma Meep right about now," she replied, then scampered away, energized by the sound of a new adventure.

"Teek, make sure you come to Colony Hall before you leave, will you?" Seek called back over his shoulder, heading back toward the Hall.

"I will, sir!" Teek called back, "and I shall be sure to report all the events of our journey upon our return." *I am in no hurry to put an end to adventure just yet,* he thought to himself.

Teek shuffled down the main hallway of his beloved, cozy burrow. He would soon be leaving it, and this time Digger would not be there to see after it. Teek had returned to Stonewood Place with several unanswered questions swimming around in his mind. As he shuffled to the back of the burrow, shafts of light interrupted the dimly lit hallway in golden pillars. The floorboards creaked in the same old familiar places, like the quiet voices of old ancestral family members. Teek stopped for a moment to feel his home around him.

His quiet moment was interrupted by a muffled scratching noise. Then a bump. The sounds then became louder. *Scratch, scratch, scratch, thump, thump.*

"Oh my!" he exclaimed in a whisper.

He moved cautiously toward the noises. Now there was nothing, no sounds of scratching or thumping. Teek stopped and stood in silence, listening, barely able to breathe, half fearing that he'd miss the next noise, but also afraid to be heard by whatever it was clawing from within his wall. As Teek stood once again in silence, the sounds resumed. Teek inched closer to where the scratching and thumping sounds seemed to be originating. He arrived at the wall at the back end of the hall. He gulped and forced himself to address the unknown. He knocked on the wall three times. The noises from the other side stopped suddenly.

Silence. He waited and waited.

Then, from within the wall, Teek heard three returning knocks. *Who or what is in there?* he thought. He decided it was time to address the intruder. Taking a deep breath, he mustered up his courage, gathered his strongest voice, and shouted "Hello, who goes there?"

A voice muffled by the wall barrier replied, "Teek? Teek is that you? You will not believe this!"

"I'm finding this difficult to believe already! Who are you?"

"This is Digger, sir!"

"Digger! What are you doing in the wall?"

"When I tell you, you may want this wall to become a door!"

"A door? A door to what?"

"A door to a passage that leads to Colony Hall!"

"Digger, did you say something about Colony Hall?" Teek asked.

Digger concluded that the best way to share the information with Teek was face-to-face.

"I will go back," he shouted. "Come to Colony Hall."

Teek heard him and replied, "No wait! We can bust through and put in a door!"

"Teek? Um... what are you doing?" Cicci had returned and scanned the operation with the judgment of someone arriving at the scene of a crime, needing to size up the situation.

"I was just busting through... uh, well, Digger is on the other side of the wall, you see and..."

"You are breaking down the wall?" Cicci continued her inquiry. "That is sort of a major project to start as we are trying to focus on getting ready to leave on a long journey, is it not?"

"Well, yes, but you see..."

Cicci looked at Teek squarely in the face. "Teek, are the satchels packed? Have you even thought about what we are bringing, or where we might be going?"

Teek stood staring at Cicci, realizing that she was, of course, absolutely right. Even though the tunnel was a major discovery and he wanted to ask Digger to join them on the journey, this was definitely not the time for breaking down walls. Digger, of course, would have had no way of knowing that.

"Digger?" he called out.

"Yes? Hello," came the muffled reply.

"I will meet you back in Colony Hall. Do not break through the wall."

"All right. I am headed back."

"Cicci, again, you are right. The fact that there is a tunnel leading to Colony Hall just on the other side of our wall, will have to wait. I want to ask Digger to join us on our journey, but I have to now go to Colony Hall to do so."

"What did you say?" she exclaimed. "A tunnel that what?"

"I cannot explain right now, dear one. I will tell you upon my return. Meanwhile, I am afraid you will have to start packing. Is Peeps going with us?"

"Oh yes, he would not want to miss it, and would have been upset if we had left without him. That is who he is, you know."

"Good. Did you tell him two cycles from now?"

"I did. He dashed into action upon hearing."

With a quick nose-to-nose, Teek departed for Colony Hall.

⸻ ❖❖❖ ⸻

S eek walked into the main hall and found Teek waiting for Digger.

"Teek, what a pleasant surprise! I did not expect you so soon."

"Oh, sorry Seek. I was looking around for Digger, but perhaps I should stay right here and wait for him."

"Digger is here? Well, no matter, he is always popping up from some tunnel, somewhere. This gives me a chance to see you before you go. There are three things to discuss regarding your journey before you go, and they are related to each other. The first one is the current situation here in the canyon, and the growing threat. The second is specifically where you are going and what you will be doing. The third is... Teek, you are to become a Story Elder. You cannot just continue to go on these adventures, risking life and limb!"

"All right, Seek, sir, let us discuss each one. Shall I address the overall threat to our canyon first?"

"All right, let us start with that one."

"The fact is," said Teek, "I do not know exactly what the threat is yet. Kanti mentioned the rats, and their encampment destroyed by the humans, but you heard that too, so you know what I know. I can guess, what might happen, but Kanti has not told me anymore than that. I will meet him three cycles from now at the Pine Stone Inn. I am guessing he will be telling me either about the current location of the rats, or the encroachment of humans further into our land, but I do not know any details yet."

"I see, so I will not know about any of this until your return?"

"It appears so, sir, and so, it follows that I also know little about where I am to go and what I am supposed to do. But I do have an idea..."

"I have a feeling that I am about to hear something quite clever," said Seek.

Teek continued, "If I keep the message simple, say limit it to our location, I could tell a songbird, and they could fly back here with it. What do you think of that, sir? Do you know any songbirds?"

"Actually, I do," replied Seek, "now that you mention it. I haven't seen him in a great cycle season, but I think I know how to find him. His name is To'ke-tie. He is what humans refer to as a Western Meadowlark. Meadowlarks have a long history that goes back to a time when humans and us creatures shared a common language. It is said that there was a time back when the earth was pure, that all living things spoke to one another. Harmony was the way of life. Then, evil spirits that wanted to destroy life, came among them. There was only one creature that could still speak to humans at that time, the meadowlark. They have always been good messengers. They have always found pleasure in bringing good news. That is why, especially early in a great cycle, you can hear them sending beautiful messages for all to hear. Mostly you can hear them sing: 'lits-tsi-pah-tah-pi-op,' which means: 'the source of life.' They sing to life itself. This bird will always bring messages that are joyous and positive, and so, include few details, be brief, and try to make the message as positive as possible. They prefer to sing about the good things in life."

"How will I know this bird when I see it?"

"You will know this bird by his bright yellow breast with a black collar over it."

"Does Kanti know this bird?"

"I think so. I will mention it to him."

"I had better call to Digger. He should have shown up by now... Digger!" Teek called out, turning toward the dark recesses of the hall chamber.

"Teek..."

"Yes..." Teek turned back toward Seek.

"The last point I wanted to make is this. Remember that your family has always been adventurous, we have lost many of them. If you are soon to become a Story Elder, you must be very careful on this journey and then, these adventures must come to an end. This colony must not lose you. You must not continue to risk your life. You have the ability to see what others cannot. You are too valuable to us."

"I believe that this journey is vital to the well-being of the colony, sir."

"Maybe so, but Cicci is right. It does not have to be you every time."

Teek peered into Seeks eyes as he called again.

"Digger!... Digger!... Digg..."

"Teek!" It was Digger, at last, appearing from a darkness in the corner of the hall.

"Sorry I took so long. I explored another passageway that branched off the main one. It led to the chambers of the Story Elders."

"You say there is a passage from your burrow to Colony Hall and the chambers of the Elders?" asked Seek. "Teek— your father! That was his passageway!"

"Yes, it must have been. I wonder when he blocked it off. Digger, this is a mystery you can definitely help me solve. For now, I have another request to ask of you. Kanti has asked that we set out on another journey that is very important to the well-being of all those who live in the canyon. Cicci and Peeps are accompanying me. Will you join us?"

"At your service Master Teek! I'd be honored."

"Good. We leave in two cycles. Pack a satchel. You will need something to nibble on for the journey. Be at Stonewood Place in two cycles, when the light of day first breaks."

6

DEPARTURE

The first light of day came early. Fortunately, squirrels are always up early, gathering nuts, berries, and bugs. There was always much to do. This particular morning was especially important as the squirrels prepared for departure. Teek and Cicci had been up before the bright light of day had peeked over the rimrock, stuffing satchels with supplies from their larder. Teek couldn't help thinking of Cheeks. With all his shortcomings, he was resourceful when it came to food.

Teek and Cicci passed each other in the hall. As cold and as dim it was, they knew they would miss the comfort of their own burrow.

"Does Cheeks know we are going, Cicci?"

"Yes, I had seen him outside one of the entrances to their burrow. I mentioned our journey. He just grimaced and waved me off with his paw. There was no interest there."

"Just as well. Peeps, then?"

"And Digger."

"Ah yes, Digger. I spoke with him at Colony Hall. They should be here presently."

Soon there came a soft knock on the door. Cicci opened the door to find Digger in the middle of inspecting the front porch area.

"We will have to replace that," he said out loud to himself.

"Digger?"

"Oh, yes Miss Cicci, Digger reporting as arranged."

"Come in and get warm. It is early and still quite cold out there I imagine."

"It is indeed."

"Digger! Are you all set, my friend?" Teek asked.

"Ready for travel, sir!"

"Now listen, Digger, we will be spending all of our time together, so you might as well get used to calling me Teek."

"Yes, Teek, sir."

"Just Teek is fine."

"Just Teek then."

"Did you happen to see Peeps out there anywhere?"

"I spoke with him early last cycle. He should be here soon if I heard him correctly."Before the bright light of day peeked over the rimrock, Peeps' momma, Meep, was up and busy stuffing food into Peeps' satchel.

"Peeps, dear, are you up? You do not want to be late. Peeps!"

"I am right here."

"Pinenuts! How long have you been standing there?"

"A while."

"I guess I'm a bit jumpy."

"Maybe you are just a little bit nervous about me leaving."

"Now be sure to listen to Tee..."

"Yes, Momma, I know, listen to Teek and be careful."

"And always watch for predators..."

Peeps grabbed his momma's shoulders with both paws and looked directly into her face. She raised her eyes from the floor and looked her son in the face.

"Momma, listen. These journeys, you see, are an adventure, and they are not always perfectly safe. I know this. You must too. We need to be brave squirrels now. I need to do this. You know this is good for me. You also know that trying to hide from danger is sometimes no safer than going out to meet it. For all of us. Is this so?"

"Oh Peeps, you are becoming a fine squirrel. I am so proud of you. You come home to me!"

"I will, Momma, I promise. Now stop stuffing things in the satchel. I will not be able to carry it! Besides, all this food is out there anyway. Where do you think we find it in the first place?"

Meep sighed and handed Peeps the satchel. With a quick nuzzle, he was off. Meep stood at the burrow door and wiped her tears as Peeps scurried down the path toward Stonewood Place.

Teek, Cicci, and Digger turned from their exchange to see Peeps coming in the front door.

Teek greeted Peeps, hinting at his tardiness. "Ah, we are all here and ready. We had better get started. I trust that you'll be able to keep up, Master Peeps?"

Steam rose from the little stream that crossed the central grassy area, and judging from their breath, it was a cold spring morning in the canyon and the sky was just beginning to show the glow of the early light. They crossed to the opening of the narrow passage that led to the entrance. The guard squirrel was on his perch above the spearhead gate, dozing.

"So long!" Teek called out loudly, with a teasing tone.

The guard was so startled that he almost fell off his perch, but then scrambled to stand at attention as they passed. Teek shot a quick amused glance at Cicci. The small company reached the outer opening of the passage and stood for a few moments, all looking at the path ahead and the river rolling by.

"Here starts the beginning of our journey. Be very careful, think of what might befall you, and listen to Kanti," Teek instructed.

Digger happened to be looking at the corner of the opening as Seek and Kanti stepped out of the mist.

"Teek." Digger nudged Teek to redirect his attention.

Seek addressed them. "The thoughts of all Rimrock go with you, my kits. Now, remember To'ke-tie, the Meadowlark, Teek. I have told Kanti here that he will bring messages back to us so that at least we know that you all are still well. You will see him first at or near the Pine Stone Inn."

"Thank you, we will look for him," replied Teek.

"I will be just ahead, downriver," Kanti said. "If there is danger ahead, I shall know. I have decided to wait to tell you everything at the Pine Stone Inn." With that Kanti launched himself into the air and flew off. The squirrels turned back to where Seek had been, but he was gone as well.

Teek addressed his group. "I guess we get started. Now, I do not need to tell you that this is a dangerous part of our journey. All the predators are out looking for us. Especially since they know there are squirrels outside the walls of Rimrock. Hug close to the bushes and the rocks, and we will make it through, and when I say ditch..."

"We ditch, yes, Teek, we know," blurted Peeps.

"Well, some of us may not. Digger is new to this, Peeps, and it has been a while since our last journey, so maybe you will be willing to hear some of this again, so that others may also know?"

"He starts right in, does he not?" Cicci whispered in Teek's ear.

They crossed the sandy slope of sage, and juniper trees, heading downriver. It was quiet in the canyon, save for the songbirds that were just stirring and beginning their early calls. The squirrels knew the language of the birds. As they continued their journey and entered new territory, they could tell they were sending the message to those further ahead, telling them the group were approaching.

"So, can the predators understand what those birds are saying and why? Because, if they can, that is not a good thing, is it?" asked Peeps.

Surprisingly, it was Digger that answered.

"Other birds, squirrels, and mice—small animals that are attacked by predators—can understand this language, but not the larger animals, or the predators. That is the reason for it, you know."

"That is right," commented Teek.

Cicci turned to Teek and made a face revealing that she was impressed. Peeps turned to Digger with surprise.

"Well, alright then. Good to know!"

They continued, Cicci sticking close to Teek.

"I do think of all those who lived in the forest around the Pine Stone Inn. I wonder what became of them," Cicci sighed.

"They are doing much better now," came a voice from above.

It was Kanti perched on a branch.

"I think he actually takes pleasure in appearing out of nowhere," said Peeps, beginning to notice a pattern.

"Hide under the rock at the base of this tree. Be quick. There is a coyote headed this way on the trail. We will let him pass. Stay still and stay quiet if you want to live," directed Kanti.

"Make sure you tell it like it is!"

"Don't start, Peeps. Everyone, do as Kanti told you and ditch into the rock," Teek directed.

Soon the large coyote trotted by. She sniffed the ground, stopped, and pointed her nose in the direction of the rock under which all were hiding. Kanti didn't hesitate. He swooped down and dive-bombed the coyote. She yipped and trotted off. She wanted nothing to do with the relentless attacks of an adult raven.

"Wait here for a while. I will tell you when it is clear."

"He is saving our hides again." Teek muttered to Cicci.

"Lucky for us," Cicci replied.

Kanti called down to them. "I will fly on ahead. Stay where I can see you."

Kabloosh! As the squirrels headed downriver there was an enormous explosion of water. They looked at each other hoping that one of them would know what to make of it. Only one of them did– Digger.

"That would be a beaver sending out a warning that danger is near," he said. Peeps looked at Teek in wide-eyed wonder.

"How does he know these things? He spends his days burrowing, right?"

"Not all the time. I do other things," Digger replied.

"I guess Digger does get around, Peeps," added Cicci.

"Well, let us all go look to see what it was," continued Peeps.

They found a small deer path leading down to the water's edge. The deep pool had a large ring of ripples and bubbles from something that had just submerged.

"Whatever it was, it is at the bottom now." Teek peered into the water searching for some movement. When he glanced back up, all the other squirrels were frozen, with their eyes fixed on the opposite bank.

A male human was standing and staring into the water. He held what looked like a long straight and very thin stick or branch in one hand. The human did not see the squirrels across the pool, he was too involved with his development to notice. He threw the stick on the ground, made a couple of indiscernible utterances, picked up the thin stick, and marched back up the hill.

"They are a noisy lot I say!" It was the beaver, still in the water, just in front of the squirrels. He was facing away from them as he spoke, watching the human climb back up the hill. The squirrels now turned in astonishment toward the beaver in the water next to them. To the squirrels, the beaver was enormous. Looking back to the squirrels, he continued.

"I guess I ruined *his* morning." The beaver had a voice that sounded like it had been sped up, yet it was not high pitched at all.

The squirrels searched for words, after a moment of silence, Digger leaned over to Peeps and said quietly, "Do you see that beaver?"

"Yes, yes, I see the beaver, Digger!"

"Hello, my name is Buzz, this is our pool," said the beaver.

"Hello... Buzz, my name is Teek, and this—"

"You're Teek?"

"Yes, my name is Teek, and—"

"Well, well, I have heard a lot about you! I thought you would be bigger."

"I am about as big as ground squirrels get, I guess."

Cicci interjected, wondering about the human, still marching back up the hill. "Mr. Buzz?"

"Just Buzz."

"Buzz, why was that human so upset? What happened?"

"Well, he came down to catch fish, you see. That long stick he was carrying is one of the ways that humans catch fish. As you know, humans are dangerous, and I do not want them ruining everything that I work so hard to build, so I sounded the alarm, you might say, and, well, the fish listen for the alarm too. So, that sort of spoiled his chances of catching anything, at least, anywhere near here."

"Are you saying that your alarm warns other animals that humans are present?"

"Yes, and predators too, like that coyote that trotted by a while ago.

She was headed somewhere and not a threat to me or my family, so I did not bother to slap at that moment."

"Yes, she was headed for us, I imagine," said Teek.

The beaver lifted his head and squinted upwards as if trying to see clearly. There in a tree sat Kanti.

"Kanti."

"Buzz."

"Is it just me or is Kanti paying a lot more attention to us on this journey?" asked Peeps.

"He seems to be," replied Teek. "It must have something to do with what he knows."

"Buzz and his family were the beavers that helped Wuchak construct the Pine Stone Inn." Kanti knew the story and knew Buzz quite well.

This story impressed the squirrels, resulting in all sorts of "oh's" and "oh my's" and "is that so's" and other expressions of interest.

"Now keep moving everyone, the edge of my forest is up ahead," said Kanti. "We must get settled into the Inn, meet up with To'ke-tie, and I need to tell you more. Buzz."

"Kanti."

Kanti launched himself towards the tops of the taller trees of his forest.

"It is an honor to meet you, sir," Teek bowed to Buzz.

"Just Buzz. My thoughts go with you on your important journey."

Peeps took note. His face showed a look of concern. "That sounds rather ominous. Do you think he knows something that we do not?"

"I am sure that he does, Peeps," answered Cicci. "He has been out here, and he pays attention enough to alarms for other creatures, so he must know, at least a little."

"Nettles! That is not good! Everybody seems to know but us!" replied Peeps.

7

A WARM WELCOME

The group reached the edge of Kanti's woods and stopped to peer into the darkness ahead.

"I know I mentioned this before, but it is so important enough to say again," said Teek, "Be very careful passing through this forest. Stay under the brush and the rocks and keep your backs to the tree trunks. There are silent predators here that strike with no warning. Although Kanti is watching out for us, he will not be able to stop everything. Oh, and this time, watch out for misguided young tree squirrels! Now follow me and be aware of what is overhead and all around. If any of you remember where to head up the slope and over the ridge to the Pine Stone Inn, speak up."

Digger spoke up. "I have been to the Pine Stone Inn. I helped burrow out some of the tunnels and sleeping chambers for Wuchak."

Teek turned to Digger. "Digger, you know Wuchak?"

"Oh, yes."

"Is there anything else you would like to tell us about yourself, Digger?"

"Not at the moment."

"All right, there was a lot of excitement when we were here last, with fire, falling trees, and looking for Cicci, so I ask for all your help directing us to our destination," Teek instructed.

The squirrels sensed something different about the forest than before. As they reached the top of the ridge, they looked out over what was the burned area.

It was almost a great cycle ago that a fire swept through, and it seemed now as though life was returning. The area was still barren, and a few charred trees remained, but there was also more activity and new growth.

Birds flew overhead and Teek could see movement in the sage bushes and bitterbrush across the way. New tufts of grasses had sprouted here and there. But there was something else, a wide pathway had been dug right through the middle of what was now a clearing. The brush and grass had been scraped away. It was now a place that the humans traveled on in those large fast monsters.

"Coming?" It was Kanti, perched on a blacked branch of a large tree.

⁂

It was warmer in this clearing at the top of the ridge. The bright light of day was now high overhead and the breeze whispered by, lightly brushing the tufts of grass, and surrounding unburned bushes. There, in the middle, to one side of the wide dirt pathway, a familiar large island of boulders remained. The Pine Stone Inn.

As the squirrels began to cross the clearing, they stopped suddenly. Kanti was about to flap over to the boulder mound when he caught sight of the squirrels below him, he noticed that they had frozen still.

Peeps looked up and explained to him. "We are not wanting to fall into a fiery pit and burn to death."

Kanti was surprised, and so made it known. "There is no more fire here, little ones, and besides, after what I tell you, fire would be the least of your worries."

"Worse than falling into a fiery pit? Terrific," Peeps said. "I would like to mention, at this point, that these foreboding comments I am hearing, that refer to terrible events... well, they are starting to get to me, Teek!"

"Well, we will be finding out soon, I should think. So just because we are close to our destination does not mean we just scramble across this clearing. Follow me."

Teek headed to the first bush ahead. As he did, *whoosh*. A large bird swept down after him, in an attempt at carrying him away, just missing him.

"Ditch!" Teek screeched. The other squirrels scampered back to the protection of rocks, bushes, and forest cover. The raptor circled back and tried again, but Teek had made it under a bush and out of reach. It was a female Cooper's Hawk looking to feed her brood.

Fwoop-fwoop-fwoop, down came Kanti from his perch.

"Croak! Kraw-hah-kkkkkk!"

"What is the matter with you!" the Cooper's Hawk screeched. "I have young ones to feed!"

"You must hunt elsewhere!" Kanti ordered. "My friend Teek is on an important journey."

"That is Teek? I have heard this name," she replied.

"I know you must have young ones to feed, but I am Kanti, the eyes and ears of this forest. I ask you to do your hunting elsewhere. This is too near the Pine Stone Inn, a refuge for small animals. This area is not a place for hunting."

The cooper's hawk explained. "I should tell you that I am from downriver, further north. There is less food there. Something has happened that has made this so. I am looking for food. It is harder to find. My mate is hunting there."

"He may be having better luck than you. There is new food in the canyon. Maybe not as fresh, but they are larger. They are not from around here. They are called rats. They come from far away. They arrived with the new humans."

"Humans!" she said indignantly. "I flew over a place where they ride those beasts that growl and blow smoke, just downriver. Quite a scene! What is happening?"

"I cannot say, exactly." replied Kanti. "Do be careful of your young ones. Nothing is safe anymore. Where the humans are is where the rats were. The rats travel in packs, and they can be dangerous, so, try to get one when it is away from the others. They are aggressive and fight fiercely as a group. Whatever you do, stay away from the humans. They have ways to harm us easily. Death comes suddenly to any who get too close."

"Well then I must go and warn my mate!" She flew off without another word.

"*Kkkkkk,* all clear little ones. But you should stay under the rocks and bushes, and not scramble out into the open."

The group of squirrels scrambled from bush to bush, and from rock to rock until they reached the large island of boulders, and the Pine Stone Inn. Then scrambling up to the top, and once again peered down at the heavy wooden door, tucked down in a hollow. There, next to the door were the familiar footprint pictograph markings of all the animals allowed to enter.

They were abruptly stopped by a bird call that came from a very near branch. It was surprisingly complicated and articulate, very high-pitched, and rather musical. It went "See-Seer-cli-cli." They all turned to see a beautifully speckled songbird with a bright yellow breast and a black bib. Kanti had been perched on a rock above them, looking out for danger. He now called down to the group.

"Oh, it is To'ke-tie. He has come to deliver the first message back to Seek at Rimrock." Kanti addressed him as he swooped down to light on a rock next to Teek. To'ke-tie sang his greeting to the group.

"Good news, good news,
for you and your kin!
You will find safety at
the Pine Stone Inn!"

"No wonder messages are simple and positive. Did you hear him?"

"I did, Peeps. He sort of sings his words. Maybe that is the only message Seek needs?" So, Teek replied. "Greetings To'ke-tie, you may take that message to Seek!"

Cicci nodded in agreement. To'ke-tie flew off without another word, or song to sing.

"I wonder what sort of song he sings when things do not go as well?" asked Peeps. "Rats, rats, they were all killed by the rats?"

"Peeps!" snapped Cicci.

"Sorry."

Teek closed his eyes and shook his head. Digger was busy examining the footprint pictographs on the rock face next to the heavy wooden door to see if they were all the same as before. Kanti hopped up to the door and knocked with his bill. The group turned and all stared in anticipation. They waited and stared some more. Then they waited some more.

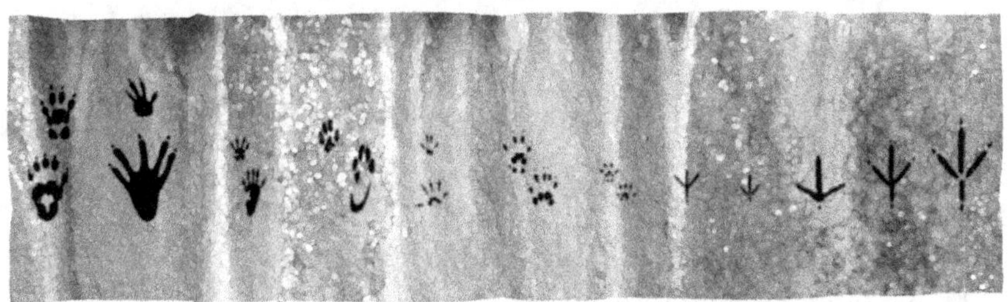

"I wonder what has happened. Are they all gone? Is Wuchak no longer here?"

Kanti turned around to Peeps. "Patience, Peeps. I think you will be surprised."

Kanti then turned back to the door and knocked again.

After some time, the little door in the large door opened, and a familiar nose twitched as it sniffed the outdoor air, and then the nose moved to one side, and a large familiar eye appeared. It rolled around, first looking left, then looking right.

"Pine nuts! It is ye all!" The big, old marmot exclaimed as he quickly shut the little door.

Kanti turned around to the weary travelers with a gleam in his eye.

"Ah, he heard us that time," said Peeps.

They all heard the familiar sound of a wooden plank being slid from the other side of the large wooden door. Then it swung open with a loud creek.

"Come in, come in! It be so good ta see ye all again! Kanti! Teek! Cicci! Young Peeps!"

"I'm a bit older now Wuchak."

"Yes, yes, so ye are, bigger too. Ye be a fine young squirrel, ye be! And who is this'n?" Wuchak leaned forward until his big friendly nose was in Digger's face.

"This is Digger," Cicci replied. "A knowledgeable squirrel from the burrow builder line of ground squirrels."

Wuchak grabbed Digger with both paws and shook him heartily. "Ah yes, Digger! Good to see you again, lad! Maybe ye can give me some pointers bout this here place while ye are here me little one."

Digger didn't expect to be shaken and was startled to the point of falling over.

"Woops lad, hold fast," said Wuchak. "Let me find you a special place ta sit ye all down." Wuchak hurried off to one end of the cavernous main room and began vigorously wiping down a large stone slab over in a corner. The travelers wandered in after him.

The Pine Stone Inn was now a busy place and quite noisy. The main cavern of the Inn was filled with all sorts of cheeps, squawks, chirps, and whistles. Jays, tree squirrels, chipmunks, field mice, robins, various chickadees and bushtits, and all sorts of other creatures filled the floor.

There was even a large beaver, as big as Wuchak, behind the bar helping out. A hum of activity and energy filled the air. The death and destruction that had silenced most of them had passed nearly a great cycle ago. Nature, if given a chance, recovers quickly. The earth has a way of rejuvenating itself. As they passed by each group, they could understand the conversations.

"… He just fell out of the nest, just fell right out…"

"... She came within a claw of that bobcat before she was able to..."

"... and they were never seen again! I think it was those rats!..."

Cicci leaned over to Teek. "Listen to all of that... it makes me think of Hiss and Chatter. I wonder what ever became of them. I hope they found a home and have stayed safe."

"They seemed pretty smart and cautious to me. I am sure they have stayed out of trouble," replied Teek.

"They have. They are well," commented Kanti, having overheard.

The old fire pit that had held a burning tree root from the fire now had large stones rolled up blocking it and sealing it off.

Cicci looked into Teek's eyes. "The Pine Stone Inn brings back good memories. I remember the smell. It's not as smoky now, but much the same as it was."

Cicci turned to Wuchak. "It is good to see such activity! I am so happy for you all."

"Yup, bout time too," he replied. "All these little ones are gettin' on pretty well, yup, pretty much. Kanti can fill ye in on the rest."

"And so, I shall, but first we need a nibble and have some pine nut brew."

"That *was* sort of a long first leg of the journey, but not as much for you I imagine, with flying and all." Peeps commented to Kanti.

Kanti, ignoring Peeps, and turned to Cicci. "I am looking forward to sipping some of that pine nut brew you promised, Cicci. Wuchak, can you bring us a big bowl of brew, and five cups?"

"Straight away, Master Kanti, straight away!" Wuchak caught the eye of the beaver behind the counter and shuffled off.

The group sat down in silence at a stone slab table near the old fire pit, looking around the cavern at the other huddled groups until Wuchak returned with a large bowl of pine nut brew, cups to dip into it, and a big bowl of assorted nuts, berries, and seeds.

"Wow," exclaimed Peeps.

Teek began– "Wuchak, we can't..."

The large marmot held up his paw, "Do not think about it! Times are pretty good round here right now, and fer what ye critters are up to, it is the least I can do. I have yer sleepin' chambers all cozy and ready fer ye. So, ye all do not worry about a thing. I will be back to check on ye."

He gave a wink to Kanti and shuffled off. Without a word, the group dipped their cups into the bowl and held them up to Kanti.

Teek raised his cup. "To all of us, and to what lies ahead."

They all drank, except Peeps, who was about to, but then hesitated and turned to Kanti. "What *does* lie ahead, Kanti?"

All eyes peered over their cups and turned to Kanti.

"Here we are again, little ones. Only this time it is not as simple as finding a stone. That was important, I do not mean to say it was not. But this problem is more—well, it is bigger. It is hard to explain, but it is a whole lot bigger, and there is more than one problem, but all those problems may be part of the same thing."

"Maybe you can just begin, and we can sort through it," suggested Cicci.

"Yes, thank you, Cicci. Well, as I mentioned to you back at Rimrock, the humans have returned now that winter is over. Apitah, the muha, and I saw them drive the rats from their encampment, killing some of them. Sleg, that big 'ol nasty alpha rat, is set on finding your village and, well, attacking it. He wants to take it over. Other animals in the canyon have been made aware of this and they intend to help, but many are predators, as you know, and would be more interested in hunting the rats of course." He lifted his wings and spoke directly to Teek. "I have learned and seen more, and I believe that it concerns all creatures who dwell in the canyon."

He dipped his bill into the cup of pine nut brew for what seemed like a long time. The others sat in silence and waited for his next words. Digger, somehow not yet shaken or frozen in anticipation, took the opportunity to join Kanti in a gulp or two of some brew. He treasured the nutty fermented refreshment.

Kanti lifted his bill and continued. "The humans seem to want to live where we all live, only when they move in, every inhabitable hole that is meant for living in, is destroyed, and cleared away. There would be no place for us, especially for you all. Yes, Peeps, I can fly." He lowered his gaze in Peeps' direction. "But I am not much of a migrating bird, so I always keep to my forest. Mind you, it is a large forest, but there is much going on beyond what even I can tell."

He paused again, not to sip, but to look at each one of them to be sure he had everyone's attention. "There is someone who tells me things, things that concern us all."

"Who is it, Kanti?" Teek asked.

"His name is Ahtūnowhiho, it means *one who dwells below*, but I know him as Ahtūn. He lives in a deep pool in a cavern in the middle of the river. He is a, a, um, 'cuuy'em.' A fish. A very, very old Bull Trout. I believe that he has a long life because he has been given some power from the Ancient One. It changed him somehow so that he would live in this world for much longer than others. I believe that the Ancient One chose him, maybe because he is hidden, maybe because he can taste and smell the water and knows what it means. He sees things that happen upriver somehow. He can sort of speak about these things. To know more, you will need to find him. I can tell you where his cavern is. He is very large and very dangerous for little ones like you. He will eat you if he gets a chance, so stay back from the water's edge. If you tell him that you know me, he will answer your questions, but he will want something from you in return. I do not know exactly what is happening beyond this, but I can tell you that the humans are destroying the canyon, and the river, to occupy it, much like the rats who want to take over Rimrock."

"How in stinging nettles were you able to get to know a fish?" Peeps asked in puzzlement.

Teek laid his paw on Peep's shoulder to settle him down. "Actually, Peeps does have a good question, but perhaps the answer is not for us to know."

Kanti answered, "You all know that I do not miss much, and as you also know, I do not stop until I find out. Might I add Teek that you are not the only one who sees the ancient one on the edge of cliffs. There is a great spirit with a force that directs us all and cares for this canyon. For those who are paying attention, the ancient one offers some direction and help. That is how I came to know of him and to meet him. There is much more to what lies below than I have seen or even know about. That is why it is so important that your journey to this cavern for the answers. You will find that the truth takes the humblest path, much like the river itself."

Teek watched Digger take another long gulp. "Digger, should you have some food to go with that brew?" he said.

He looked back at Kanti, adding, "If there is more to learn about what lies below Kanti, it is good that Digger is with us."

"So, you say that the other creatures in the canyon might help? We did learn about how important our community of creatures is on our last journey. I do not think that we can do this alone," Cicci said, and then thought some more.

All the others were silent in anticipation.

"Perhaps this Meadowlark—what is his name? To... To..." She struggled to pronounce it.

"To'ke-tie," Digger managed to say between gulps of pine nut brew.

"Yes, To'ke-tie—thank you Digger—maybe he can send more messages than just those meant for Seek?"

Teek stared at Digger in disbelief, partly for his ability to remember such a difficult name, partly in amazement at his love for pine nut brew.

"Maybe this To'ke-tie fellow," Cicci continued, "can send messages, with help from other birds to other creatures in the canyon. From what you say Kanti, much needs to happen all at once. We cannot do it all. Once we find out what is happening, we could just get the creatures of the canyon in one place, and we could ask for their help. We could all work together to protect our homes. We all need to unite, even with the predators. Maybe for now, we might just put a hold on predation!"

Teek responded. "Yes, that is good, that would work, Cicci. A very good idea. We find out what Ahtūn knows first. We must keep the message simple and sort of *singsong* for To'ke-tie, but when you think about it, all To'ke-tie needs to relay is that it is important for there to be a gathering of those representing their type of animal because their home is being taken. Yes, that could work... Kanti?"

"That seems to me to be a good idea. Cicci, you are right, many things need to happen at the same time. I can help To'ke-tie find the other animals."

Wuchak arrived at their stone slab table shortly and slid a special bowl in front of Kanti. "And a special plate of grubs and worms for you Kanti, me lad."

"Oh my, Wuchak, that does look good. Eat up, everyone." As Kanti looked up from his bowl to begin, he noticed that everyone had already begun eating. "Well, it appears that a long journey is good for the appetite."

"Are you Teek?" came a voice.

Teek turned his head to reply, but nobody was there.

"Are you Teek?" the voice repeated.

This time, Teek looked down, and below him, looking up, was a small field mouse.

"Oh, excuse me, I did not see you there. Yes, I am Teek. May I help you?"

"You already are helping, sir! I could not keep from overhearing, and talk has been traveling quickly. I am Pip, and I want to make myself available to help. I can spread the word about your gathering of animals farther than you might think."

"Well, Pip, I am most grateful for that. All creatures of the canyon are welcome to help. Once we know what needs to happen, I shall send word back here to Wuchak."

Pip bowed respectfully to Teek. "We are at your service, Master Teek." With that, he scurried off.

"Talk does travel fast. I think maybe that will be a good thing when the time comes," Teek concluded.

Once all had finished eating and all the pine nut brew was gone, it was time to sleep.

Kanti took a moment to prepare them for the next day. "It will be at the first light of day when we must get started. Adventure and danger lie ahead. You should all find your sleeping chamber now. I am headed for the treetops."

"How do you get any sleep up there Kanti?" asked Cicci.

"Oh, I find a crook in a tree and clench the branch, and we ravens are light sleepers. In case something happens below in the middle of the night, we do not want to miss anything. We are the eyes and ears of the forest and cliff tops. But you all have a busy day tomorrow."

8

—————————

LEAVING A LEGACY

"**G**randpa, are you awake? Grandpa?"

Sofia found her grandpa asleep in his easy chair. Walter awoke and opened his eyes. He had journeyed to another world and was just returning. "Sofia, dear," he reached out his hand, and she held it.

"I was unable to wake you up. You scared me."

"I was far away. I'm back now."

"Where were you?"

"He was visiting with his ancestors, I imagine," said Nute in a quiet voice.

"Yes, that is right. I saw my mother, father, and my grandparents. Who is this, Sofia?" Walter gestured toward Nute.

"This is Nute."

Sofia bent down and whispered in her grandpa's ear, so that Nute couldn't hear.

"Do you remember the boy I told you about?"

"Oh, the quiet one? Yes. Everyone is speaking of him on the other side. Everyone seems to approve."

"The family approves of him? Well, that certainly is good news, and unusual. Things must be different on the other side," she replied.

"Hello, my name is Nute."

"Nice to meet you, Nute. Have you been awakened, too?"

"Sir?"

Walter looked at Sofia. She grimaced and shook her head quickly.

"Sir?" Nute repeated.

Walter looked longingly up at the ceiling and called out, "Mother, is that you?" He then turned and winked at Sofia.

"He speaks to ancestors from the other side," said Nute.

Sofia decided that Walter needed some fresh air.

"Shall I get your wheelchair and take you out to the front porch? We can all sit and watch the sunset. May I get you anything, like maybe some tea?"

"A cup of hot tea would be very nice," Walter answered.

Nute opened the front door and Sofia wheeled Walter out to his front porch. Just beyond Walter's red lava gravel driveway, the view stretched out for miles before them. From the front porch there was a vast valley of juniper and sage, with one or two groups of ponderosa pines. The valley eventually sloped up to the dark shadowy pine forests of the Three Sisters Wilderness Area, a remote part of The Cascade Range.

The evening light cast a golden glow on the old cabin porch as the three sat quietly in a row, feeling, and smelling the soft evening air, the remnants of another beautiful and toasty warm day in Deschutes country.

Walter took a deep breath, drawing in the taste of the land before him. "This air has calories."

Sofia recognized this comment and acknowledged it with a smile and a pat on her grandpa's back.

"How's your mother?" Walter asked, separating himself from fatherhood.

"She's doing fine, Grandpa. She's working part-time in that dress shop you know."

"Ah yes. Is she still seeing that—"

"Ah, no. That didn't work out."

Sofia's answer came before Walter had a chance to finish asking, as though to quickly change the subject.

Walter responded anyway. "Pity, he seemed like a nice fellow."

Nute sat in silence. He knew that Sofia needed time with her grandpa, and he also knew that listening is always better than talking.

"A beautiful evening, isn't it?" Walter began. "So quiet this time of day. I saw your grandma, Elisabeth. She has finally forgiven me, and she's very happy, and doing quite well."

"Grandpa, she passed on over a year ago."

"Yes, yes, I know, but she is doing well, and she is much younger now. She likes your young friend, Nute."

Sofia glanced at Nute. He shrugged with a little smile as if to say, *Sure, why not?*

"Well, I..."

"Enough small talk, Sofia. How are our friends in the canyon?"

"Grandpa, you know I can't talk about that!"

"Hasn't your young friend here been awakened yet?"

"Grandpa please, I would like to, maybe soon."

Nute's eyes turned slowly toward Sofia and Walter. He raised his eyebrows. *What is all this?* he wondered.

As if hearing his thoughts, Sofia said, "It's nothing Nute. I'll tell you later." She closed her eyes and shook her head slowly.

"I'll look forward to that..."

"So, what's happening?" continued Walter, "It was a long winter. It has been too long since I've heard news."

Sofia answered. "I don't know very much yet. I need to find them. We've been down there once. I was going to tell him then, but..."

"But what?"

"Well, I forgot to bring a tapping stick."

"Sofia, that's like arriving at someone's home uninvited, or not calling them first to see if it is a good time to show up. Always bring a tapping stick."

"I will, I will. Anyway, I didn't go to the village. Next time."

Nute's eyes turned and stared at Sofia and Walter revealing his search for answers, their exchange was a little puzzling to him. Although he did wonder if they could possibly be referring to the animals in the canyon.

Sofia quickly changed the subject. "Oh look, it is turning into evening, Grandpa. The sun is just barely peeking over the Middle Sister, and it's starting to cool off. Are you getting chilly, Grandpa? Do you need a blanket?"

"Nute, can you go in and grab the blanket off of the couch and bring it to me, son?" Walter asked.

Nute sprang to his feet and headed inside. Walter leaned forward and looked intently into Sofia's eyes.

"How's Teek and Cicci?"

"They are doing well together. They have departed Rimrock again. I hear that Kanti had something they need to do, something urgent, but I'm not sure what it is yet."

"And Kanti? I want to know about the raven, Kanti!"

"I don't know his whereabouts at the moment, but I do know—"

Nute returned with the blanket. Walter and Sofia stopped talking suddenly.

As Walter draped the blanket over himself, Nute spoke in his usual way of few words. "What did I miss?"

"Nothing I can share with you at the moment, Nute. It is difficult to explain. In fact, it will be difficult to explain even when the time is right," Sofia replied.

"You may be surprised. I've heard many things in tribal meetings that many people would think are unusual."

"Well, this one can never be spoken of. Grandpa, how are you getting along? Do you need anything?"

"Oh no, I'm able to get about with my cane, and Trudy comes in every day to clean and cook and, you know, check-in. She's pretty amazing. She's so handy. She takes on projects I wouldn't have tried even when I was young!"

"Well, you're lucky to have found her, Grandpa."

"I just wish I could visit my friends in the canyon again. I would very much like to get back down there next to the river just one more time."

Sofia placed her hand on her grandpa's shoulder. "Well, there's no reason why you can't get back into that part of the canyon, even if you just walk across a bridge. I may be able to get you close. I do know someone who would love to see you."

"Who?" asked Nute.

Sofia held up an index finger.

"Teek? Oh, I do miss my little friends. I kept one of the tapping sticks you know…"

"Who's Teek? Tapping sticks?" asked Nute.

"I'll explain later."

Nute dropped his head and stared at his shoes.

"We'll get Trudy to put you in your pickup and find a good spot." Sofia assured. "It may not be right at the place you're thinking of, but at least I can get you close so you can smell that fresh canyon air down near the river…" She paused. "And you never know. Maybe I can find someone that can tell our friends where you are."

"Tell who?"

Sofia's eyes shot toward Nute. He quickly gathered that it was not the time for any more questions.

The sun had dropped behind the Cascades, leaving only the glow of the valley on the other side, a valley still busy with activity. The evening sky gradated to deep dark blue revealing the twinkle of the first evening stars.

"It sure is a beautiful evening, but I should probably go inside and settle in. Maybe have a nice hot cup of tea."

"Yes, Grandpa. Nute and I should probably get going. Tomorrow is Saturday and we'll have to get an early start."

"An early start?" asked Nute.

"Yes, an early start down into the canyon. You want all your questions answered, don't you?"

"Well sure, I just didn't know—"

"It's best to just take it as it comes, son." Walter gave a wink. "You probably know by now that this one doesn't waste any time thinking about what she wants to do."

"I think about what I want to do, I just don't take very long!"

Nute and Walter shared another little glance.

"Well, I should settle in for the night." Walter turned his old wooden wheelchair toward the door. "Help me in. Hey, how are you getting home?"

"We brought our bikes, we're not far."

Nute knew he'd have to wait until morning for the answers to his questions.

54

9

THE CAVERN OF AHTŪNOWHIHO

The first light came early. Although not much light made its way into the cavernous Pine Stone Inn, Teek followed his usual internal timeclock and was up before the others. Good 'ol Wuchak was up early as well. He lit a little fire using sticks and pinecones in a pile of rocks in the middle of one of the stone-slab tables. Teek sat quietly, nibbling on crumbled nuts and berries. Presently there was the rap of a bill on the wooden door. Wuchak shuffled over quickly.

"That would be Kanti, I figger!"

He opened the little door to peer out first, just to be sure, and then let Kanti in. The chill of the early day also came in, but there was no wind, and it would be a beautiful bright blue-sky day ahead.

"Greetings Kanti. I will go wake the others."

They all filed into the room, blinking their eyes, and wiping their faces with their forepaws. Digger was the last one down the passage from the sleeping chamber, his eyes were still shut as he crawled toward them.

"How do you suppose he can find his way over here with his eyes closed?" asked Peeps.

"They are not all-the-way closed," replied Digger. He felt it was a bit too early to have to explain himself.

"Eat quickly dear friends, we start soon," announced Teek.

"And so it begins," Kanti said as he pulled up to the table. "What wondrous things lie ahead for you all, little ones."

"I wish he would stop referring to us as *little ones*! It isn't exactly a confidence booster," said Peeps.

Kanti began again. "Alright my *brave* little ones, I must fly back upriver toward Rimrock and locate To'ke-tie. I will share Cicci's idea with him, I'll try to keep it short. He can then start sending messages to the other creatures in the canyon, and I will come back to find you, and begin looking out for you from above. So, while I am gone, be extra careful. I will not be here to look out ahead or tell you when to ditch in advance. You will have to rely on your own caution and quickness. But you know all about that."

"We are good at that!" Peeps declared.

Teek addressed Peeps, saying "The stakes are high Peeps, so do not be too confident. We must be extra careful. It will be all our jobs to use our senses and to stay alert. It will be all right to shout 'ditch' even if nothing ends up happening. Do not hesitate!"

"Gather your satchels, everyone. It is time," said Kanti.

The group adjourned and headed up the tunnel for their satchels. Wuchak made sure to stuff a special packet of something to nibble on in each of them, saying "Ye'll be need'n this along the way, ye will. Now ye be careful dear ones, we all will be thinkin' of ye, alright."

Once all the appropriate "farewells" and "safe journeys" were said, they were ready to embark.

"Thank you Wuchak," Teek stopped and embraced the marmot. Almost getting lost in his thick fur, he said, "It is always good to know that you are here. Your hospitality and friendship have meant so much to us. I do not know what we would do without your hospitality."

Wuchak patted Teek, then pulling away the wooden beam, he opened the door, and the group stepped out into the crisp morning air.

"Your attention, please. All of you," croaked Kanti. "Listen to me while I tell you the way to find the opening of the tunnel to the cavern of Ahtūn. Remember, I will not be with you to guide you, but you are all squirrels of great abilities and sensibilities. Stay sharp, remember my words, and you will be all right. Remember one thing very well. Finding Ahtūn is only the beginning, but you will learn much more from him. But know this, be very careful. He would rather eat you than help you."

Kanti then described their next leg of the journey with the sort of detail that ground squirrels appreciate. They had been that way before, only headed in the opposite direction, and higher up under the base of the rimrock cliffs. The direction Kanti now described was a deer trail down near the bank of the river. But one thing was very clear, the cavern lay at the base of the rockslide that covered the burial chamber of the ancient human. A massive talus would be the most noticeable feature that would guide them.

Kanti had a few more words before his departure. "I cannot say for sure how long I will be, but once I have delivered my message to To'ke-tie about announcing the gathering, I shall return. I may see Seek. If so, I will fill in more details of your journey and what lies ahead. Do any of you have anything you would like to say to me before I lift off?"

"Hurry back?" suggested Peeps.

"Anything else? All right then, close your eyes." He jumped into the air, and they could feel the now-familiar dust, sand, and other little bits kick up, blown by the first three beats of his powerful wings. He disappeared over the crest of the pines and headed south, upriver.

Teek turned to the group. "All right everyone, as with every time we travel early, I will tell you that this is the time when predators are out hunting, so be especially watchful. We need to stay as much under the brush as possible, from cover to cover. Here we go."

They reached the edge of the burned clearing and peered over the edge toward the river.

"Teek?"

"Yes, Peeps."

"I heard a human voice."

They all froze under the cover of large sagebrush and sure enough, there, walking along the bank on the very deer trail that they were looking to follow downriver, were two adult humans, a male, and a female. The squirrels were unable to make out what they were saying, but they could hear the sound of them speaking to each other. The male made grand gestures, pointing this way and that, holding up both hands to reference that which he sought to direct the female's attention to, which just happened to be up the hill toward the squirrels and the outcrop of boulders that held the Pine Stone Inn. The squirrels stood frozen for quite some time, waiting for the humans to move on, but for some reason, other than moving a few steps this way or that, they remained focused up the hill in the direction of the squirrels.

Cicci looked around at the others. "Does anyone understand what they are saying?"

They all shook their heads.

"Maybe, for now, we shouldn't try to find out what they are saying and just go way around them. I would add though, that something does trouble me. Maybe it is an intention that I sense."

"I sense the same thing, Cicci," said Teek. "It is understandable to be concerned when humans start pointing at your home, but I think you are right. We need to keep moving."

With that Teek scampered to the next cover, heading down the hill. The others followed, giving the humans no sign of their presence. Although somewhat closer to the humans, the squirrels were now well hidden, and so, able to pick up a couple of words.

"The female human has just mentioned rats. Listen," said Cicci. They all stood perfectly still and listened.

"—because I don't want a bunch of rats crawling around, black, grey, orange, striped, or any other kind!"

"Yes, yes," said the male human, "we'll take care of that."

"She does not look like she is from around here," Cicci added.

With that, the two humans headed upriver, and the squirrels headed downriver, sticking to the deer trail.

"I wonder if this is such a good idea, Teek," she began again.

"Why is that Cicci?"

"Further upriver, on this trail, we encountered a coyote. Now we find two humans talking about rats, and maybe talking about us. Also, Kanti is not with us to look out ahead. Do you think that maybe we should move off the trail, as long as we do not lose it?"

"Yes, I agree. Listen everyone, this way. The going might be a bit more uneven and a bit steeper, but possibly less out in the open."

They climbed over boulders, underbrush, and around the roots of trees. Digger brought up the rear, paying close attention to anything that might be coming from behind. The light of day was now overhead and the sandy soil beneath their feet was getting toasty warm.

"Let us stop under that large boulder up ahead, cool off, and see what Wuchak stuffed in our satchels," Teek suggested.

Once under the boulder, Digger spoke. "I have been here."

"That," said Peeps, "does not surprise me."

"You have been this far from Rimrock?" Teek asked.

"Yes. Two seasons ago."

"How far. This big slope of boulders?" asked Peeps.

"Yes, I have been as far as this big talus, up ahead."

Peeps corrected himself. "Or... I mean, talus! Do you know what is under it?"

"No, I do not. More rocks?" Digger asked.

Peeps was pleased to hear that there was something he knew that Digger did not.

"Well then, you're in for a surprise," said Peeps. "At some point, I should at least tell you all about it."

At this point, Peeps had determined that Digger knew a great deal and was somewhat of an adventurer himself.

"What did you do when you got here?" asked Teek.

"I turned around and came back."

"I see. Well, this time we are going to keep going."

Which they did. Following Kanti's direction, they headed down to the base of the talus. They could see the enormous vertical boulder that Kanti had spoken of. They concluded that it very well could be the entrance of the passage to the cavern of Ahtūn. The large boulder of lava towered like a monument. It had the look of a portal to another place. It stood as though it had always been there, redirecting the flow of the river around it. Its smooth polished sides covered its many massive faces. The bright light of day lit up the green marshy cattails and tall blades of grass on the other side of the river. Above them, swarms of salmon flies flapped their wings, giving off sparkling flashes of light. A light, sweet breeze picked up and rustled the tall green blades at the water's edge, blowing the flies about. Some landed in the water. Large trout rose to the surface to slurp them up. It was the first day of the hatch. These were the promising signs of the beginning of bountiful days.

Not unlike many spots along the river, thousands of years ago these large boulders had tumbled down the slope to the bottom of the canyon and into the river.

"Look here!" said Peeps. "Looks like a pathway through the brush." And, so it was, through frequent use, there was a round tunnel hollowed out of the thick brush from the frequent use of creatures that were roughly as big around as otters or beavers.

"Must be an otter path" Teek said hopefully.

Deep down he wondered.

"It does look as though it might go in the right direction," said Cicci. "It is worth a try. I do not see any other way through to that rock if that is the one that Kanti described."

They moved single file through the thick brushy tunnel, hoping that they would not come across an unexpected traveler like a weasel, martin, or some other predator returning from the riverbank. Arriving at the tall boulder, they noticed that the brushy tunnel continued to the riverbank. At the base of the boulder, a dark opening looked like the beginning of a tunnel or burrow. To the right side, not visible to those walking by on the trail above, there was a pictograph. The type of image, the reddish color, and its quality were very familiar to the squirrels. Digger stood before the large pictograph without making a sound, staring in wonder at the image. It was masterfully rendered. There was no mistaking what it was. If it was life-size, it was a very large fish. Finally, Digger spoke:

"What do you suppose that is? It looks like the tracks on the wall of the Pine Stone Inn."

"Well, it looks like a large fish to me," Teek replied.

Here is the image they saw on the rock face:

"Well, this tunnel... or burrow is marked with this image, so this must be the place." began Peeps.

Cicci, then spoke. "Teek, what if I were to stay just inside this opening with Digger? You and Peeps can take a look. If this is the place, you can retrieve us. If it is not, come back and we will continue looking. If something in the brush concerns us, we will come let you know."

They all agreed that was a good idea. Teek and Peeps turned and headed deeper into the tunnel. It sloped downward toward the river. Presently, they could hear the rushing, gurgling, and swirling sounds of the water echoing off the walls of the tunnel and noticed that there was a hint of light emanating from an opening below them. The air was cooler through the passage and held a strong smell of wet stone walls, water plants, and a strange fishy sweetness. Teek and Peeps stopped suddenly in their tracks at the opening at the bottom of the tunnel. They stood before a large cavern that had been hollowed out over the eons by the relentless force of water. The rocks were smooth and shaped in curves. Just before them, at their feet, was the subterranean river. Tens of thousands of years ago the river had been covered over by an ancient lava flow, and over those tens of thousands of years, the river had worn carved out deep hidden pools. They peered in wonder and amazement into the greenish blackness of the deep swirling abyss. Against a wall of rock to their right a whirlpool made a slurping and sucking noise as volumes of water were pulled deeper into unknown caverns.

"You fall in there and you will probably never be seen again, young master Peeps, so please watch your step," warned Teek.

Water poured into the cavern through an opening in the rock at the up-river end of the ceiling. Through it came a shaft of light. It shown down on the surface of the pool, illuminating the dark waters. Bubbles swirled and foam collected against the stone face at the other end of the pool. The light from the opening in the rock where the water poured in, lit the cavern enough for them to see the opposite wall. There, positioned on a ledge just above the waterline was an enormous amber-orange and bronze crayfish with large and imposing red claws. The crayfish was glistening as if it had just crawled from the water. Its antennae waved up and down, and its stalk-like eyes dipped in and out of its shell to keep them wet. Teek and Peeps stood frozen, eyes fixed on the intimidating crustacean.

"It cannot make it over here, can it?" whispered Peeps.

"I do not think so" replied Teek quietly.

"So, what do we do now?" asked Peeps.

"I am not sure, and I am not sure we should try to find out," replied Teek.

So, there they stood, staring at the crayfish. The crayfish turned and faced them as if it knew they were there and began clacking its claws, the sound echoing off the walls of the cavern.

Teek leaned toward Peeps saying, "I think it is trying to get our attention. What do you think it wants? It sort of looks like it is supposed to be there for a reason."

"Say something to it," prodded Peeps.

Teek turned and stared at Peeps, then his gaze returned to the crayfish. "Wait one moment. What if this creature is like a guard or a sentinel of some kind?"

"Hello, you there!" Teek's voice reverberated, sounding much larger than it was. The creature reared up and lifted its claws. It was an imposing sight for the two squirrels. Both were grateful to be on the opposite side of the deep water. The enormous crayfish turned around and faced the smooth wall of dark lava rock behind him. Teek and Peeps looked at each other again in puzzlement and then back to the crayfish as it began to tap the wall with its enormous claws. Each time it did so, a deep ringing sound resulted, almost like an iron bell. One, two, three, then a pause, then one, two, three, and another pause. This pause was longer than the first pause.

Then it began again, one, two, three, a pause, then one, two, three. *Bing, bing, bing* it went. The sounds reverberated throughout the cavern in such a way that the squirrels could feel the vibration in their toes.

"How very strange," said Teek.

"That is one way to put it," replied Peeps.

The crayfish turned back around to face them.

"Okay, that was very... unnerving," Peeps concluded.

Teek nodded but was staring into the water. His eyes had gotten wider.

"What?" asked Peeps.

"I am not sure. I thought I saw something pass by us down in the water. It was enormous. There it is again!" He lifted one paw toward the pool. "Did you see that?"

"I did, it *is* big."

"Maybe it would be a good idea if we backed up a bit from the edge of the water and back into the opening of the tunnel." Teek began.

Just as they did, the water exploded as a massive maw clopped together. An enormous fish surfaced and lunged at the two shocked squirrels, sending them scurrying back into the opening of the passage. Then the fish re-submerged with a splash, back down into the bubbling, swirling watery darkness.

"Wow! Peeps, are you alright? That fish *was* big, bigger than any I have seen... Peeps? Peeps?" Teek turned to where Peeps had been positioned next to him, but he was gone. Peeps was scrambling back up the tunnel. "Oh my, oh my, not good, no, no," he squealed as he scrambled.

"Peeps! Peeps!" called Teek. "Come back!" But Peeps was well on his way to the opposite end of the tunnel. Teek turned back, gathering his wits. The leviathan had returned to the surface. Its enormous back and dorsal fin slid by Teek's astounded stare. Teek kept his eyes on the water as the fish turned and circled the pool. This time it glided up and stopped just under the surface to stare at him. The eye was the size of Teeks largest wooden pine nut bowl. It rolled as it examined the missed meal. Slowly the fish rose until its head broke the surface. It was shiny and dark green with lighter spots. Then it made a sound, more like a gurgle than a voice, so quiet that Teek wasn't sure whether he was really hearing it or feeling it.

"I am Ahtūnowhiho, One Who Dwells Below. I almost got you. I should have gotten you. How did you escape? Where is the other?"

"He ran back up the passage," replied Teek.

"Why are you still here?"

"I was told to come here to learn from you, and I was warned of the danger."

"So, you knew that I would strike?"

"Yes."

"Who is it that told you this? How do you know of this place?"

"Kanti, the raven, told me to come here. He is my friend. Do *you* know him?"

"I do. Kanti has eyes and ears above. I can sense things that are below and beyond. We share what we know. So, you are a friend of Kanti's?"

"Yes, I..."

As Teek was about to begin his lengthy explanation of his relationship with Kanti, the giant fish submerged and sank back down into the dark depths, as if to brood on the matter. Teek stood, not quite sure of what was to happen next. He lifted his eyes to the opposite wall of the cavern to check on the whereabouts of the crayfish, but it was gone. Teek stood alone in the chilly, dimly lit cavern with only the swirling and sucking sounds of the flow of water echoing off the walls of smooth stone. He had concluded that the moment had arrived for him to return to the others to discuss the next move with Cicci, when he began to see movement once again from the depths below, as the massive fish began to slowly rise from the blackness.

Ahtūn lifted his head from the water again and opened his massive jaws. Water spilled out as he began to speak in the same quiet, almost indiscernible gurgle.

"What did Kanti tell you?"

"Kanti told me that you know of things that are beyond... far away... upriver. How is this so?"

There was a long silence, and then, as though a voice was traveling through time, he spoke again. Teek could hardly believe what he said.

"I can taste the water that I breathe. It brings me visions from far up the river. When I taste the river, I can see what is happening. The river connects us all, all that live and depend upon it." The creature then slipped below the surface again. Teek settled down a bit and waited for the great fish to resurface.

Soon it rose again, bringing its entire head out of the water. Its eye rolled again as it looked Teek over, noticing that he stood nearer the water's edge. Teek couldn't help but wonder whether he was being sized up for a possible second attempt at a meal or if Ahtūn was merely getting a better look at him.

"What is your name?" it gurgled.

"My name is Teek."

"Teek," it repeated, "sounds tasty. What do you want to know, Teek?"

"I want to know what you see. I want to know what is happening upriver. I want to know what lies beyond. Can you tell me anything?"

"What you want is much. What I see is much. What I know is hard to explain."

"If you describe to me what you see, I will try to understand."

"Oh, you will do more than that. You will bring me those large, winged creatures flying around on the surface to eat. You will do this, or you shall go no further."

"Further? Is there more?"

"Much more. But you will never know unless you do as I ask."

"I will do as you ask. What do these winged creatures look like?"

The creature that Ahtūn described to Teek was what was hatching with abundance and flying over the cattails and reeds at the edge of the river in the midday sun. Humans might refer to this creature as a type of stonefly common to the river—referred to as a salmon fly (Pteronarcys californica). To the humans it meant great fishing. It was the easiest time of year to tie on a big fly and catch a large trout. In early spring, when the salmon flies turned from larvae to fly, the feast was on. This large-winged insect, almost as long as Teek's tail, was a prized source of food to the ground squirrels and fish alike. In the world above the cavern, they were swarming in abundance, but out of reach to the one who dwelled below.

"You will bring me many of these creatures. Only then will a reveal more," Ahtūn instructed.

"If I bring you a satchel-full, will you tell me what I need to know?"

"This satchel you have, is it big enough to hold many?"

"It is large for us," replied Teek. "It *should* hold many."

Ahtūn almost seemed to choke on the water as the words spilled from his mouth. "I want them alive. They need to be alive."

"Yes. I shall return with them shortly."

Ahtūn submerged and sank to the bottom.

Teek crawled back up the passage, this time taking close note of the size of it. The ceiling appeared to be high enough to allow a creature the size of Kanti to move through it. Is this how Kanti came to visit this creature? Kanti's obsessive curiosity would certainly have drawn him to want to acquire knowledge from Ahtūn.

As Teek continued back up toward the top of the passage, it occurred to him that it might be a good idea to pay closer attention to the surroundings. His senses and his attention now more tuned in than when he had descended, he carefully examined the walls and pathway as he made his way back to the world above, back to his friends, back to the light and the warmer fresher air.

He stopped halfway up at a point where the passageway took a bit of a turn. It was at this spot that Teek caught a sudden draft of warm air coming from the wall and a slightly different smell. He stood before what appeared to be the mouth of another passageway. He and Peeps had missed this earlier when they had been heading down toward the cavern. Most likely because they had been focused on what unknown fate might await them at the end. *Maybe this opening was not meant to be seen while traveling down the passage,* Teek thought.

On further and closer examination, the outline of the opening began to reveal itself. A dim light from the entrance above highlighted its edge, then it immediately dropped off to a dark and unknown destination. All was silent. He drew closer and peered in. Through the depth and the darkness, echoing from an unknown origin, he heard something.

Could it be? He had heard this before. It was so quiet, he wondered if he actually heard it or if his own mind remembered this sound from another dark unknown opening. Teek could feel his heart pounding in his chest. It was the same ever so distant slow and steady beating of a drum.

Teek stood in front of the passage as his thoughts wandered back to the burial chamber of the ancient native human. He began to put it together and make a connection. He realized that what seemed like two different and separate experiences may very well be linked. He decided that he needed Cicci's help to figure out what it meant. He continued his climb out of the passage to its opening and rejoined the other squirrels.

Going nose to nose with Cicci, he reassured her, and himself, that he was alright.

Cicci spoke quietly to Teek. "Peeps told us of the monster down there. Is that Ahtūn?"

"Yes. Yes, it is."

"Will he help us, or does he just want to eat us?"

"Both actually. I believe he will tell us everything that we need to know, and I believe that he is the key to continuing our journey, but we need to fill one of these satchels with the large flies and bring them to him."

"Just that?" asked Peeps. "That is all he is asking for?"

"Yes. Remember he dwells below. This is most likely a rare delicacy for him, and certainly that giant crayfish cannot catch any for him."

"That giant what?" Cicci asked.

"Oh, did Peeps not mention the crayfish?"

Peeps shook his head. "I did not really get a chance."

"Ahtūn has some kind of sentinel or guardian down there that taps on the stone and announces visitors. You will see."

"Oh, I can hardly wait," Cicci replied.

"I shall empty my satchel into each of yours so we can use it to fill with salmon flies. Digger, Peeps, leave your satchels here and start gathering flies."

They returned shortly with two flies in each paw and one in Peeps' mouth. *Crunch, crunch, crunch.* "It was too good to resist." A wing hung out of one side of Peeps' mouth. He stopped crunching long enough to offer a sheepish smile.

"Peeps? Will you and Digger go gather four more please?" Teek opened the satchel bag, while Peeps and Digger stuffed the flies in.

"We will be right back with more. They are everywhere, and crawling all over the bank."

"Be careful not to get too close to the water, you two," Teek warned. "I have seen fish flop themselves onto the bank after frogs, and young ducks and geese. I am most certain that they can do the same for a ground squirrel!"

"Cicci, I—Cicci? Where has she gone?"

"Two more," she said as she reappeared, and stuffed them in the satchel.

"Oh, good. Thank you."

"We were only able to grab two more each," said Digger, as they returned, flies in paw.

"That is all right, I think we probably have more than enough." Digger and Peeps shoved the wriggling bugs into the satchel.

"Quick, close it up." Teek pulled the drawstring, and they were ready. "Pick up the satchels and then we will get started again. Everyone, stay close behind me."

Peeps replied "No problem with that! You can definitely go first. I am just fine staying behind you! Cicci, wait till you get a look at this."

As Kanti approached Rimrock, he could see To'ke-tie perched on the top of the Rimrock cliffs, peering down into the village, getting ready to fly back down river. Seek, and two other ground squirrels were with him seeing him off with final words.

"One moment please, To'ke-tie, I have something important to send with you."

"Welcome, welcome
You are most welcome!"

Kanti landed and began to convey his direction.

"Thank you. We need to spread the word quickly, to all the creatures in the canyon, that we are calling a gathering the night after two cycles. Can you do this? Is there enough time? We need only one or two representing each type of creature. Then those two need to tell their own kind," Kanti explained.

"Spreading the word
to all the creatures
A gathering is called
from the large black bird
A request for all"

"Well, not all, we would like only one or two to represent each creature," Kanti continued.

"Yoo-hoo, yoo-hoo
A gathering is called
We only need two"

"So, that would be two per creature, so that they can spread the word to their own kind, and then they would need to know that the gathering would be in two cycles," Kanti further explained.

"A gathering, a gathering

two cycles from now
two creatures are welcome."

"Look, I can help you with the message, let us just get started. If any of them need to know more, I will tell them. The important thing is that we get started. You fly downriver and I will fly up, then I will come back and find you." Kanti shook himself, as though to rid himself of the confusion.

"You fly up and I fly down
If you need to know more
That is what Kanti is for
And he'll circle back round"

Kanti stared in silence at To'ke-tie for a few moments. After some thought, he shook himself again and said, "All right then, off you go."

To'ke-tie flew off downriver, which was a good sign because Kanti wondered if he had heard anything, or if he was able to retain anything.

"May the spirit of the canyon go with that one," he croaked to himself. "May it go with all of us!"

1 0

IT TAKES A TOLL

The squirrels traveled single file down the dark tunnel toward the cavern. Teek was in front with the satchel filled with salmon flies. They moved cautiously and silently. The only sound was the rustling of the flies and their shuffling feet, which seemed to echo off the walls of the passageway. Soon they could make out a dim light coming from the bottom of the tunnel, from the cavern of Ahtūn.

As they approached the cavern, Teek stopped and turned to the group. He stopped so suddenly that Cicci, second in line, bumped into him, then Peeps bumped into her, and Digger bumped into Peeps. Once everyone had stopped and gathered themselves, Teek spoke quietly.

"Please, everyone, pay very close attention. Do not get ahead of me and always stay well away from the edge of the water. Ahtūn will look for an opportunity to grab you, pull you under, and eat you, but as long as you stay behind me, you are safe."

Peeps pondered for a moment and then said, "So far, I am really not all that sure of what you consider to be safe."

Teek looked in Peeps' direction. "Peeps, please do not panic and run, just stay back."

Then Digger spoke up. "I would like very much to be closer so that I can see you give the fish these flies!"

Peeps replied "you say that now! Just wait until you see him."

Teek called back, "Peeps, will you let Digger pass so that he can get closer?"

"Sure, go ahead," said Peeps, "but do not say I did not warn you."

Digger moved into position behind Teek, and they approached the opening to the cavern. The shaft of light entering the cavern from where the water spilled in, illuminated their view.

"Wait here," Teek ordered. He moved closer to the opening.

"Teek, may I come closer, if I keep behind you?" Digger asked.

"Yes, come along, but be ready, when I tell you to ditch, do as I say."

Digger peered across the deep pool to the far wall. There stood an enormous crustacean with huge red claws.

"What is that? Is that Ahtūn?" Digger asked.

"Oh that, Digger, is only a crayfish. It is the one who summons Ahtūnowhiho from the deep. It will use those claws to 'ring the rock' and call him to the surface."

Their voices resounded off the smooth walls of the chilly, dimly lit cavern, mixing in with the sound of the deep, dark, clear green, swirling water, bubbling and gurgling by. Digger watched it swirl by them, then stared in astonishment as the water was drawn deeper down at the other end of the pool, and into a black whirlpool. It made a sucking sound as it swirled under the massive wall of stone and into the abyss.

"This must be the strangest thing I have ever seen."

"Yes, you do not want to fall in, Digger. We would never see you again."

The crayfish turned to face them. It waved its antennae and raised its claws to signal them, then it turned like some armored machine toward the wall behind it.

"It sure smells wet and strange down here," commented Digger.

"You will forget all about the smell very soon," Teek replied.

The two squirrels' attention was drawn back to the crayfish suddenly as it knocked on the wall behind it with one of its giant claws. As it did so, a deep ringing sound resulted, the iron bell sound from before. one, two, three, then a pause, then one, two, three, and another, longer pause. Then it began again, one, two, three, a pause, then one, two, three. *Bing, bing, bing,* it went.

"What is it doing?' asked Digger.

"It is summoning Ahtūn."

Digger watched as Teek stared into the deep water.

"Look there!" Teek pointed his paw toward the surface of the swirling darkness. Digger turned away from Teek and redirected his gaze to the water in time to catch a large shape slip by.

"Oh my, he is bigger than I thought. Magnificent!"

Teek searched for answers in his mind to Digger's comment.

"Did you mean to say… frightening?"

"It is thrilling to be on this journey with all of you and see such things, Teek. Thank you!"

"Prepare yourself," was all Teek could say.

As before, the water exploded as Ahtūn sounded. The eruption of water slapped against the stone ledge where they stood, drenching the two squirrels in a wave of cold river water. They stood, dripping, staring straight ahead.

Finally, Digger spoke. "Well, that certainly got my attention."

The water lapped up all around them.

"It appears that the water is higher than it was last time," Teek noticed.

"Oh, all right, do you think we should move back a bit?"

"Maybe so."

Cicci and Peeps were some distance back, but they could still see the goings-on at the opening to the watery cavern.

"I tried to tell them. Now they are soaking wet." Peeps paused in thought and then continued. "I wonder why Kanti has not joined us yet?"

"He has much to do Peeps," Cicci answered, "and perhaps this cave and tunnel searching would be too difficult for him. We spend much of our lives burrowing and tunneling. Kanti spends much of his life flying, or in the treetops, or perched on cliffs. He *has* come to visit Ahtūn, but he has not explored as we must. I have a feeling that there is more for us to discover down here. Maybe Kanti knows that, and so, has chosen to leave that part up to us."

Peeps nodded but didn't reply as the two squirrels began backing into the tunnels.

As they did, Ahtūn raised his enormous head out of the water and rolled his large, shiny, bulbous eye to search for the squirrels. *Clop, clop, clop,* his jaws snapped shut to clear the water from his throat. He gurgled and croaked and then spoke, again, in barely discernible words.

"Are you leaving, Teek? Who is with you? Is it the one who fled before?"

"No, that one is further up the tunnel. I have brought another. His name is Digger. He is a master at navigating through tunnels."

"You will need him. Did you bring me what I asked?"

"We did, oh mighty, Ahtūnowhiho. What would you like us to do now?"

"If you can, let one out of the bag at a time. If two happen to be released, that will be acceptable. Lower your satchel to the water and release them onto the surface. Do not worry about danger young squirrels. You are friends of Kanti, and I will only eat the flies you brought."

"And you will tell us what we need to know?" asked Teek.

"You are a wise one. Kanti has chosen friends well. Yes, I will tell," he gurgled.

Teek untied the satchel strap and placed the opening at the water's edge. A single salmon fly emerged, flapping on the surface of the water. Before either squirrel could watch the fly lift from the water, *slurp!* It was gone.

The great fish surfaced. Splashing water echoed through the chamber.

"You can release one after the other I will catch each one in turn."

Teek released the next one, and the next, and the next. Each was slurped up in turn.

"I want more."

"More?" Teek asked with surprise. "We agreed that one satchel would be enough. How do I know that, once I bring you more, you will then tell us what we need to know?"

"Where did Kanti tell you to find out what you need to know?" asked Ahtūn.

"He told us to come to you."

"And so, you have. I will tell you enough, to let you know that you have indeed come to the right place." With those words, he submerged.

From behind them, they heard Peeps ask, "More flies then?"

Teek held up a front paw.

Presently, Ahtūn resurfaced. The two squirrels stood very still and listened carefully as the great fish spoke in soft gurgles. Few had heard or could hear for that matter, what they now heard. The Cavern of Ahtūn was connected with two other caverns by tunnels or passageways. Both of these caverns were on their side of the river, including the burial chamber of the Ancient One, the first human, a native shaman that had brought the Illumination Stone to the colony of Rimrock. One passageway afforded a way to get to another cavern. Teek strongly suspected that the opening to the other passage further up the entrance tunnel led back up the hill to the burial chamber, but what that had to do with all of this was unknown to him. He also strongly suspected that he needed more answers.

"Now, I have told you enough so that you should understand and believe that I will tell you the rest when you return with more flies. I only want one more satchel full of them."

"Then we shall gather more and return."

"More flies then?" repeated Peeps.

"More flies, Peeps." Teek then turned to Digger– "go with him to gather more if you would please."

Teek and Cicci followed them both up the tunnel. When they arrived at the outer opening, they noticed that while they had been in the cavern, the light of day had moved over to the other side of the river and was heading toward the mountains to the west.

Cicci noticed first and commented, "We need to begin to think about where we might hole up until the bright light of day breaks over the rimrock again."

Peeps and Digger were just returning with more salmon flies.

"We will deliver these first," said Teek. "This passage starts out a bit wider up near this entrance. It is not ideal, but it is safer than out in the open. Maybe we deliver the flies to Ahtūn and bed down in here, then we can get a good start at the first light of day. We will huddle together to stay warm."

He turned to Digger. "Come with me, Digger. I need to bring more flies to Ahtūn. We shall see how well he keeps his word."

The two headed down the passage, returning to the cavern. Arriving at the opening to the cavernous pool they found it to be much darker than before, as the bright light of day was now lower in the sky. They could still make out the crayfish on the opposite ledge. It stood quite still, rigidly waiting for their return. It then turned and tapped a large claw on the stone wall, like ringing a bell. Ahtūn rose from the depths like before.

"You have returned," he gurgled. "You do what you say you will do?"

Teek confirmed this was so. "Always."

"Then you shall know more and go further."

Teek released the flies onto the surface of the pool with flutters that sent radiating ripples. With splashes and slurping sounds, his great jaws clopped closed on each fly. After each time he disappeared below the surface. When the last fly was consumed, Ahtūn resurfaced.

"You have gained my trust, Teek. I will now tell you more."

"We must first rest, mighty Ahtūn. May we return at the first light of another cycle?"

Ahtūn floated motionless in the water. His large round eye rolled as he thought. "The flies should be out in great numbers when the light of day lands on the water of the river."

Teek looked over at Digger and then turned back to Ahtūn. "With more flies then?"

"Yes, yes, more flies!" Ahtūn's eager gurgle echoed through the cavern.

"How do we know you will...?"

"You have gained my trust. Now you must trust *me*. It is your only hope of going further."

"He has a point you know," Cicci whispered. "We are not likely to go further without his help. Besides, we do not want to upset him."

Teek sighed and lifted his gaze to the ceiling in thought.

"Alright. In the morning, we will return with one more satchel of flies. We shall want to know more and be on our way!"

Ahtūn slipped below the surface without a sound.

Teek turned to leave, whispering to Digger, "Keep your claws crossed."

A NEW GUARDIAN

Nute sat on the front porch at first light. It was cold on the upper plateau. The small ranch house where he lived with his mother, Kaya (short for Kaya'aton'my) and grandfather, Joe, was at the end of a long, red lava, gravel road. The ranch house was small, but it had been in their family for three generations and included a corral and a barn. It was nowhere near water, save for the well. Although there were a couple of other small ranches on the road, it had always seemed to Nute as though the road was their driveway.

Nute's great grandfather had acquired the small ranch back in the days when they were giving out allotments.

Since Nimiipuu only had one name, it posed a problem because the white man needed two names for a person to acquire property. Not only was finding another name a bit of a problem, changing a name was a big event in one's life. It required a ceremony. Nevertheless, Joe's father, Kiyiyah, or Howling Wolf, got through it and the family was able to start a ranch, although times were very lean.

Nute and his family could always tell ahead of time when someone was approaching. In years past, it was a warning and gave them time to defend themselves. This morning it was a welcome sight. He could see Sofia on the road, peddling on her bike toward their house, the red dust billowing out behind her. There was something very purposeful about her approach. Was she headed toward something or headed away from something? Backlit by the early morning sun, her arrival was just ahead of schedule.

"Here she comes, mom."

Kaya, Nute's mother, leaned against the front door jam, with kindness in her eyes saying "Okay dear, have fun. Let me know how it goes. I'll tell your grandpa you have gone."

"Tell Grandpa I've gone to talk to the animals."

"You what?"

"Never mind."

"Okay, have fun with your new friend."

Nute hopped up onto his bike and they peddled off together, heading back out the red lava gravel road, without a word spoken. He glanced over a couple of times, mostly without turning his head. Sofia was clearly preoccupied with something. Nute was not one to press or demand a 'good morning' from her. This time, he did, however, offer one.

"Howdy."

"Yeah, morning."

"Are you okay?"

"My mom didn't come home last night."

"You were alone? You should have called me."

Sofia glanced over with a complex mixture of emotions. Nute realized that the best way for him to help was to just be there if she needed him. A wise decision, and probably one of the reasons that Sofia was so fond of Nute. Other boys spent too much time talking about themselves. Sofia talked enough for both, and Nute always knew he could learn more by listening.

After a long enough time had passed, he spoke. "I don't know what a tapping stick is, but I thought I'd mention it because it looks like you have brought one."

"Yup, there it is. I'll show you how it works when we get to the bottom of the canyon."

They found the old, bumpy, dirt road that led to the trailhead and followed it to its remote end at the edge of the rimrock. Sofia hopped down, leaned her bike against a tree, and untied the long cloth bundle. Unwrapping it, she revealed a long narrow, stained, and polished stick with strange pictograph and petroglyph-like markings, several precious translucent stones, arrowheads, strange carved figures and other artifacts embedded in it. There was also a feather floating from a strap at the top.

"That is beautiful, Sofia. It looks like it holds magic."

"In a way, I guess it does. C'mon then, I have something to show you."

They scrambled down the switchback trail with youthful anticipation. The trail branched out just before a landing above the river. The chilly morning air hung over the river like a heavy blanket. They stood quietly and watched the wondrous scene before them. Large trout rolled on the surface of the dark steaming water. They breathed in the sweet sage and lush spicy brush that clung to the banks. They listened to the breeze, filled with the language of birds. Some were musical chirps and whistles some were more raspy screeches harkening from prehistory.

There was always a King Fisher with its rattling, chattering call, echoing off the basalt rimrock walls, speeding up and down the banks. One call that Nute noted, Sofia found particularly funny. It sounded like they were being laughed at. It was a canyon wren. This was just the kind of thing that she needed to renew her spirit and bring her back to the world she loved, a world filled with natural sounds, smells, and wonder.

Without a word, Sofia headed down the upriver trail. "We'll stop up here first."

Nute was a nurturer, and so he felt that it was a good time to offer up some nurturing. "You know what I like about you, Sofia?"

"No, what?"

"I like that you walk through the canyon-like a gracious visitor. Most non-native people walk around like they own the place!"

"Nobody owns this place, Nute. Nobody!"

They stood for a few moments and looked at each other. No words were spoken. Nute was moved to smile. His heart seemed warmer when he was with her. Sofia was something special and he knew it.

"This way," Sofia directed.

They traveled quietly and carefully down a narrow deer trail. Very soon, eyes were peering at them from the tops of boulders, just up the slope from them. Sofia knew they were being watched. What she didn't know was that Nute also knew they were being watched. Sofia glanced over as they called to her. To Nute they sounded like the normal squeaks of the golden-mantled ground squirrel. But Sofia could hear them call to her.

"Sofia! Look! It is Sofia! Go and tell the others!"

"Sofia!"

Sofia continued walking as if she heard nothing.

"Those squirrels are making quite a lot of noise this morning," commented Nute knowingly.

"Aren't they though?" Sofia replied coyly.

"They almost seem as though they are calling to you."

"Do they now?"

There was a long pause and then Nute continued. "Are they?"

"Are they what?"

"Are they calling to you?"

"Just a bit further, Nute."

Nute smiled to himself. They came to where the trail made a sharp left around an outcrop of rocks, and here Sofia stopped. There were some flat boulders positioned almost in a circle.

"Let's sit here," she said.

They each chose a boulder and sat quietly. Sofia stared at the rimrock cliffs above them, then she tapped three times on the stone next to her. Then she tapped again three times. Then she waited. Nute stared at her.

"Sofia, I..."

Sofia lifted one finger, stopping Nute from continuing, and pointed toward a boulder. Three feet away, there was a small figure perched on top of it. There stood Seek.

"We heard you were coming," said Seek.

"Yes, we heard you all chattering too."

"Chatter? Who's chattering?" asked Nute.

"Seek, would it be possible to awaken Nute?" asked Sofia, "I'd prefer that he didn't think I was a little crazy."

"I don't think you are crazy."

"This is Nute, Seek."

"Nute? Is that his name?"

"Not all of it. That is what I call him."

"I think I know this human. He is a native human?"

"Yes, and he is my friend. He is here to help me…" She turned to her friend as a thought crossed her mind. "Nute! Aren't you wondering why I am talking to this squirrel?"

"Not really. I mean I don't understand him, but I know that it is possible. My elders speak of it."

"He has story elders, as we do?" said Seek.

Sofia looked at them both and wrinkled her brow.

"Well, maybe I should just leave this up to you two."

"You have chosen well Sophie. I feel that he will be a good companion and a good ally for us. Tell him to look at me."

"Nute, would you look at the squirrel please? His name is Seek. He, too, is a story elder."

Nute looked down at Seek. The second he did, everything changed. Voices. Voices from another place, but it was this place from which he was being called.

"Ipsusnute… Ipsusnute."

"I hear my name!"

"Someone is calling out Nute?" asked Sofia.

"No… my real name… Ipsusnute, who I really am."

"Yes, it is I, Seek. Calling to you, Ipsusnute. I know who you really are."

Nute looked at Sofia with his eyes wide. "It is true, he speaks to me!"

Sofia couldn't help confirming what she had already felt. "I knew that you could be awakened, Nute. You had the spirit of the natural world already in you."

"Yes, you are also a descendant of someone very important to us," added Seek.

Seek could see that Nute had descended from a long line. A line that reached all the way back to The Ancient One in the burial chamber.

"There are no accidents. This is one of the truths, maybe one of the most important truths," said Seek.

"What are you talking about Seek?" asked Sofia.

Nute answered. "He already knows, Sofia. He knows who I am."

"Who are you?"

"I am Ipsusnute."

"Yes, I know."

"I was given this name after my great-great-great-grandfather. He was a holy man, a very special spiritual human, a shaman. His name was Ipsusnute. Somewhere down here, he rests for eternity. It is said that, during times of great need, he shows himself in spirit form to protect the creatures of the canyon."

"No way!" Sofia shoved Nute in the chest. She was amazed and impressed. "Why haven't you said anything to me about this?"

"Oh, I guess I needed some more to go on myself, I needed to know more about you, your grandfather, and…" His words trailed off.

"Yes?"

"Well, you know me. I don't speak much. I mostly listen. You do enough speaking for both of us."

Sofia shoved him again. Nute knew it was a shove of love.

"Next time you have something that important to say, you tell me!"

"I'll try. None of us know exactly where he is though."

"I bet I know someone who knows where he is."

Seek had been listening to the exchange intently. Now he spoke up. "Because of Teek, I know where he rests, and so does Kanti."

"Who is Teek and Kanti?" asked Nute.

"You will see them soon," Sofia replied.

1 2

THE RIGHT OF PASSAGE

Teek awoke early. The four squirrels had slept curled up together for warmth, and when Peeps stretched in his sleep, he nudged Teek awake. Teek felt the cold spring morning breeze flowing in through the opening of the passageway. The fresh, early smells of the canyon flowed in with it. He turned to Cicci lying next to him.

"Cicci, Cicci!"

"What is it?" Cicci rolled over and snuggled close to Teek, still half asleep.

"Let us get outside into the bright light of the early day and get warm."

"Oh... yes. Yes, all right."

They found a small clearing of dusty, sandy ground surrounded by the thick brush. The ground was beginning to warm and was lit brightly. Cicci's eyes were still half shut, and she blinked in the brightness. To Teek, gazing at her glowing fur, she was just as pretty as the first time he ever saw her.

"How are you, dear one?" he asked.

"Ready for a nibble and a sip of something," she replied, in a familiar tone.

"Let me see," Teek went on, "we have to collect more flies, then bring them to Ahtūn. There's good water in the cavern, you could eat one of the flies."

Cicci's eyes leveled sternly at Teek. "I think it may be a bit early for flies, dear."

"Ah, yes, of course. I will go get one of our satchels and see what we have."

"I think Wuchak stuffed some berries in," Cicci called after him.

Teek turned back to her and stood gazing at her in the bright light of the early morning.

Cicci opened her eyes wider as if to say, *well, do it then!*

Teek found Peeps and Digger still sleeping, using the satchels for pillows.

"All right, both of you. Time to go."

Teek lifted one of the satchels letting Peeps' head drop to the floor of the passage.

"I am up now." Peeps scrambled to his feet. Digger awoke and rose as well.

"Grab a quick bite," Teek instructed. "Then we need to gather another satchel of flies for Ahtūn. His cavern is where we pick up our journey. I will be outside in a clearing with Cicci. I would not like to come back in here to wake you up again. Can you follow me out?"

"Right behind you, Master Teek," replied Digger.

Peeps rolled his eyes and chuckled in judgment.

"Mind yourself this morning, Peeps," said Teek.

Once outside, Teek handed the empty satchel to Peeps and spoke to them.

"There should be a good swarm of flies this morning, out where the bright early light is warming the banks. I think if you..."

But Peeps and Digger had scurried off down the hollow toward the river, relishing the challenge before Teek could finish his instruction.

"Watch for predators, be ready to ditch!" Teek called after them. "Listen to the birds, they sound the alert!"

Peeps and Digger had disappeared around a bend. Cicci was rummaging through the other satchel.

"Ah, here they are! Wuchak put some salmonberries in. How thoughtful!"

Peeps and Digger had almost reached the riverbank when quite suddenly the silence was interrupted by an explosion of wings as a flock of quail took to the air. They had been startled by the sudden pounce of a predator. A coyote was on the hunt for the first meal of the day. Coyotes are opportunists. They need to be that way, to survive. They are a very resourceful creature.

"Nettles!" chirped Digger.

"Ditch!" screeched Peeps.

The two squirrels dove between two stones just under some bunch grass, just before the coyote trotted by.

The coyote instinctively stopped and turned his head in the direction the squirrels had just gone. But his mouth was full of quail, so he turned back and kept trotting.

"Did you see that? He got one of those birds!"

"That makes us safe," added Digger.Peeps looked over at him and contemplated the natural laws of survival.

"Yes, well... indeed... better that one than us," he said looking at the coyote trot away, then glancing quickly back at Digger for further confirmation. They carefully collected flies, maintaining a level of alertness, and returned to Teek and Cicci.

"Did you see that, that... what are they called?" puffed Peeps.

"Edza'a," said Digger.

They all turned and looked at Digger.

"That is what I have heard them called anyway," he explained.

"You do not miss a thing do you," Peeps replied, adding– "well the Edz..."

"Edza'a" Digger repeated.

"It must have just missed you two! It got one of those birds!"

"He must have headed straight up the hill, not noticing us here in this little clearing," replied Cicci.

"It probably headed back up somewhere to eat it. Did you get the flies?" Teek was focused on the task ahead. Peeps handed him the satchel, stuffed full of wriggling salmon flies.

"Good. Well done. Is everyone ready?"

"I could eat something," said Peeps, "the flies made me hungry! How about you Digger?"

"Sure, I will have some," replied Digger.

"Yuck," said Cicci, finishing a berry.

Teek answered. "Hurry. I will start down the tunnel with the satchel. Be quick about it, we need to go back down together."

Cicci and Teek headed for the passage.

"Have you eaten?" Cicci asked.

"No."

"You should eat something."

"I will." Teek glanced back. "You have leg in the corner of your mouth, Peeps. Let's go everyone."

Down the passageway they headed. Teek kept an eye on the right wall of the stone passage as they descended toward the cavern. Passing by the opening, a gust of warm air blew from the blackness. It had a stronger smell than before, a smell that Teek and the others could only compare to rotten eggs. They had smelled this before, when an egg had fallen from a nest, broke on a rock below, and baked in the sun. Listening carefully at the passage entrance, he could just hear the quiet echo of drumbeats from deep within.

"Do you hear that sound, Cicci?"

"I am not sure. There is something I hear, but I am not sure what it is. It is so quiet, it seems to go away and come back."

"I hear it continually. It calls to me. We will return here soon; I am sure of that."

This was a tunnel that Teek knew that he would be returning to. What he didn't know was when, and why.

The group resumed their descent toward the cavern, which became cooler as they approached the pool. Soon the dim light from the cavern started to appear, far enough away to still look small, at the end of the passage.

"Not too far now, almost there," Teek assured everyone.

As they peered from the darkness of the passageway into the cavern, it was much brighter than it had been before. The cavern almost glowed with the bright light of day, now positioned to shine directly into the pool. It illuminated the waterfall pouring in from the opening in the rock on the upriver side of the cavern. With it came a watery breeze from the surface of the river. Beams cast across the water that moved much like the lights beams they had seen at night, at certain times of the year, far off from the direction the humans lived. Crystalline bubbles swirled around the pillars of light in the illuminated clear green swirling water. Lifting her face to the ceiling Cicci watched the light from the surface of the pool, dance in waving and rippling patterns against the smooth stone surface.

"That is something to see, is it not?" whispered Teek to Cicci.

"Something to see, it is, but something tells me that we should not be drawn any closer to the edge, Teek, we should move back a bit." The glorious new view of the cavern captivated the squirrels until their attention was broken and redirected toward tapping coming from the opposite wall. It was the crayfish.

"Is that thing trying to get our attention?" asked Peeps.

"It appears so," came Digger's reply from behind him.

"Well, either it is on some kind of schedule or Ahtūn must be hungry." Peeps became nervous, and so, chattered incessantly. He stared into the pool. "It looks deeper than I thought it was. That goes way down deep. What was that? Was that him?"

"The crayfish has not announced us yet, Peeps," said Teek. Ahtūn does not know we are here. Everyone, please step back."

Teek held out his forepaws to usher everyone back. As before, like the precision of a swiss watch, the crayfish turned and tapped with one of his oversized claws, on the rock face behind him. It made the same bell sound– *bing, bing, bing,* then a pause, then again– *bing, bing, bing.* The resonance was so great, they could all feel the vibration in their toes.

"Teek... I am... I have to admit, now that I know what is down there, I..."

"I know Peeps, this is the scary part."

Peeps and Digger had continued staring into the water, searching for any sign of the leviathan.

"Wait, this time I think I really see something!" claimed Peeps.

"This time you may be right," confirmed Teek.

Just then Ahtūn emerged, with a gush of water. He clopped his jaws together, expelling water from his gills, and gurgled his words.

"You have returned. I am hungry for the flies. Have you brought them?"

"We have, mighty Ahtūn." Teek answered. "Here they are."

"Drop them in the water and I shall grant you information and passage. One among you doubts my words. Remember, we are *all* looking to you little ones, to keep us safe. I will help you to do this. Do not doubt me."

All the squirrels turned and looked at Peeps.

"What? I didn't say anything!"

Teek stepped towards Peeps. "You did not have to. It is not unlike you to pass judgment before it is due. If we are betrayed, dear Peeps, it is not as much our loss, as it is the loss of the one who does the betraying."

Teek's words were wise. He sounded as though his words were someone else's.

His face even caught the attention of Cicci, now looking at him in wonder.

"Teek? Teek?" She grabbed him and gave him a little shake. "Teek!"

"Yes, yes, I am here. What happened? Where was I?"

"The words you spoke did not sound like you."

"What did I say?"

"Whatever it was, Teek. It was perfect. I understand," said Peeps.

Teek stepped to the edge of the pool and released the flies, one by one, onto the surface. As soon as the flies began to flap their wings, they were slurped up by the jaws of Ahtūn.

When Ahtūn had consumed all the flies that Teek had presented, he lifted his massive head out of the water.

"Thank you, little ones."

"He is beginning to remind me of Kanti," Cicci whispered into Teek's ear, but Teek's attention remained fixed on Ahtūn.

Ahtūn explained how important the feast was to him. "Simple pleasures become even more pleasurable. I do not take them for granted, as time goes by. Look to your right, there should be a narrow ledge. No one has passed this way since the ancient one made himself small enough to do so. Now, you may go in peace. This passage leads to the way across the river."

The squirrels glanced at each other in confusion. Then, all eyes returned to Ahtūn, with the hope of learning more so that they might understand.

"At the end of that ledge is an opening in the rock that leads to your next destination. Be careful to not slip and fall in. If you do, you will be sucked down deep into the whirlpool and never be seen again. So, be very careful. Do not fear me now, you may pass without my strike. You have proven that you can be trusted to carry out this task that lies ahead of you."

"Task ahead of us? Why do I keep getting these feelings of foreboding?" asked Peeps. "Everyone keeps making references to 'what lies ahead!'"

"Peeps, please!" Teek squeaked.

Ahtūn submerged.

13

ACROSS THE RIVER

"Is that it, then? Did Peeps make him mad?" asked Digger.

"I think he will return. He may be simply breathing," Teek replied.

"So that is what he is doing," concluded Cicci. "He is breathing! Fish need to breathe in the water! That is why he submerges!"

"Well, there may be other reasons, but I think it may be mostly that."

Soon, Ahtūn resurfaced. Water ran off his shiny, smooth surface and poured from his massive jaws.

"Clop, clop. At the end of the ledge," he gurgled, "near the whirlpool, you will find an opening to another passageway. That leads you to your way across the river to the other shore."

"What does all this mean, Ahtūn? What is happening?"

Ahtūn submerged again. They waited.

Peeps wasted no time. "My guess is that this answer is going to require a lot of breathing before he begins."

"Possibly so, Peeps."

After some time, Ahtūn lifted his head out of the water.

"Here is what I know, but there are some questions you may ask that even *I* do not know the answer to. I *do* receive messages. Some of my messages come from the water itself, I can smell it and taste it. This brings me visions of things beyond our canyon. Other messages come from birds. Not all creatures can understand the language of birds. Birds can go almost anywhere, and they tell each other what they see and hear. They hear the humans, and they understand, some more than others. Some birds, like Kanti, understand most everything they see and hear, and help other creatures to know. He and others like him, go to the places where the humans live. They bring these things back to me. The river itself is part of me. I have lived a long time. That is because of the spell from the ancient human. He also gave me abilities to see beyond, he is the key to this canyon. He controls its fate. He is now in a realm none of us understand. There is a burial chamber..."

"We have been there," said Teek.

"You have seen him?" asked Ahtūn.

"I have."

"Has anyone else that is here with you seen him?"

"No, just me. But in our village, our story elders say that they have seen him."

"And the passageway? There is a passageway. He placed this in my head so that I can see it. Do you know this tunnel?"

"I think so, the opening is up this tunnel behind me, about halfway, is it not?"

"Yes, it is."

"So, tell us Ahtūn, what is happening? What do we do?"

Ahtūn had already submerged, breathing, not deep, just under the surface and watching the wavy watery group of squirrels peering down at him from above the surface. Soon, he resurfaced.

"There are more humans. There is more every day. I can smell them. They are upriver. They take the water from the river. The river changes because of them. It tastes different... not fresh anymore. Sometimes there is more water, sometimes, so much less. Also, the birds, like Kanti, tell me about the rats. They are moving through the canyon. The humans do not like them, but they do not understand that they brought them here. I have not caught a rat yet. I hope to try one, but I hear from the muhas that they have a strange taste. The humans attack the rats, it is said that they want all of them gone, and these humans I speak of see all of you squirrels as rats, just another kind. Other creatures like marmots and mice, they also see as rats. They do not want you here. They do not want any of us here."

"But this is our home; this is where we live!" Cicci exclaimed.

Ahtūn's large eye rolled around trying to identify the new voice; then he submerged.

"Maybe he only wants to speak with you, Teek," Peeps noted.

"I do not know. Maybe you are right."

"I am sorry, I did not mean to interrupt."

"It is all right, Cicci, he is probably just breathing."

After some time, Ahtūn resurfaced.

"There are two places that the humans are destroying in order to occupy. One place, the rats lived in black tubes..."

"We have been there, and we have seen it," inserted Teek.

Ahtūn continued. "There is another place they want to destroy. Back upriver there is a place that burned. It is a place where many small creatures gather and find safety. It is a place where a marmot is in a large mound of boulders."

"Wuchak and the Pine Stone Inn, we have just come from there. Wuchak is our friend. Tell us what you know about this."

"I only know what I have been told. There are two humans that have been coming to that place. They have been overheard talking about what they are planning. There is a female human and a male human. What we know is that the female human is from somewhere else far away. She wants all of you gone. The male human will try to trap you or poison you. He will try to kill you, and everyone in your colony. Somehow you must prevent these humans from taking over our canyon. You are supposed to learn how to do this. You go now to a gathering of canyon creatures."

Ahtūn submerged again.

"How does he know all this?" Cicci asked.

Ahtūn resurfaced, and Teek asked another question. "Do you also know what *will* happen?" asked Teek.

"No. But I have learned that saving the canyon is why you are here. It has something to do with the ancient human. The one who is now in spirit form."

The squirrels looked at each other. Peeps shut his eyes. He knew there would be great peril and strange times ahead. Digger's eyes were open wider than ever. *This will be a great adventure,* he thought to himself.

"There is one other thing; I do not know what this means, or what it has to do with any of what I am telling you. I smell something else in the water. It smells... rotten. I told Kanti. He has smelled it too, he says it is like a bird's egg that has fallen from a nest, broken open and spoiled in the sun. I do not know what it means. It does not seem to be from the humans upriver. Now go into the passage at the end of my pool, which will lead you to where you will cross the river. The rock ledge along this pool is narrow. Do not fall in, if you do you will not come out again, you will be sucked down, and there I will have you. But do not worry little ones, if you do not fall in, I will not harm you. I want you to fulfill your destiny. Farewell little ones. Our thoughts and hopes go with you."

"Good gravelly grit! I am not sure I want to fulfill *my* destiny?" muttered Peeps.

"Is everyone ready then?" asked Teek. "Do we have our satchels with us?" The three stuffed satchels were held up.

"Alright then, follow me."

The narrow ledge pathway was a challenge, it was just above the surface and wet from the splashing of the water, it was slippery and almost too narrow to traverse in places. Teek imagined that this ledge may even be underwater at times. They tried not to look at the swirling depths next to them. This was a part of the pool that darkened as it was sucked under by the swift current.

Eeek! A loud squeak rang through the cavern. Digger had slipped and narrowly escaped falling in. He scrambled quickly to regain his paw-hold. Teek spun around, almost falling in the water, himself.

"Whoops!" exclaimed Digger, with a little smile.

"Whoops?" repeated Peeps. "Really? Whoops? Whoops, there goes Digger, sucked into the depths, never to be seen again? Oh well, I guess we lost one! WILL YOU BE CAREFUL?"

"Alright, alright, I am still here, Peeps!"

"We are almost to the opening, keep moving. Are you alright, Cicci?"

"Right behind you," she assured him.

Teek waited until everyone had entered the opening of the passage before he turned and continued. The passage was not completely dark. There were small cracks at the top where the boulders didn't quite fit together. Light filtered in, providing a dimly lit view of the way ahead. Mist and spray from the subterranean waterfall floated through the shafts of light. All around them they could hear the rush of water. At one point they entered a wider part of the passage where there was a ledge and a dark chasm to one side. Below them was a thunderous roar of a waterfall, in a tone that sounded like pouring water into a tube.

"Do not look down. Keep moving," Teek encouraged.

"This sure does not feel like a great place for a ground squirrel," said Peeps.

"I think it is wondrous!" declared Digger.

"I always thought you *liked* adventure, Peeps," said Cicci.

"I am not so big on waterfalls and deep water. This is a bit, well, how can I put it? Too... powerful... too perilous?"

"Well, soon we will be on the other side of the river, and this will all be a memory. Hey, you have never been on the other side of the river, have you, Peeps? None of us have!" Cicci's words, intended to refocus Peeps, were a revelation for all of them. Then she added, "So, there is a way across the river? I wonder how we will return."

None of them had thought about the way across, and certainly not the way back.

Teek could only say, "Well, we shall soon see, will we not?"

Cicci answered with, "Yes, I imagine that we will... just something to think about."

Soon they came to an opening. It was more of a stone dock than anything. There, perched on a stone ledge, was the crayfish.

"Look Teek, the crayfish! The same crayfish!"

This lobster-sized crayfish positioned itself on a rock on the opposite side of the dock where the squirrels had gathered for their ferry ride. It was motionless except for its antennae and eye stalks, yet it was about to call for their ride across the river. To the squirrels it seemed almost mechanical, as if it were being controlled by something or someone else.

The four squirrels stood on the stone dock and thought about what to do next. The crayfish knocked on the stone wall beside it, with a large claw. Then it knocked again. Soon from downriver, a floating branch moved purposefully upstream toward them. Under it was a large floating flat piece of bark. Out in front of all of that was an otter. This otter pulled this makeshift ferry with ease, as if there was no drag at all.

"Amazing, look at this." Peeps could hardly believe his eyes. "This has to be our passage to the other side!"

With expert maneuvering, the otter pulled the floating raft right up to the stone dock.

"Hello there," said Teek, "Thank you. Shall we climb aboard?"

"I will pull you across. Hop on."

This otter was all business and got right to it, with very few words.

On they all hopped. Onto the bark and under the branches. The bark was low in the water, which came over the bark where they stood. It was a very unsettling feeling and caused them to grab onto the branches above.

"Hold on" said the otter. "And stay away from the edge. The otter held a rather thick harness in her teeth and headed out across the pool, pulling the raft behind her.

The squirrels could feel the power of her swimming as she pulled the raft out across the pool into the deep water. They couldn't bear to look off the edge of the bark into the swirling deep water all around them. Their only comfort was the constant tug of the otter pulling them across.

"Now, this is an adventure," declared Digger. "Our past is behind us, and our unknown future lies ahead of us. How exciting!"

"I appreciate your enthusiasm Digger. Well said," Teek acknowledged.

All eyes were on the approaching shore. A large flat rock provided another dock for their raft. The approaching shore of solid ground was a welcome sight.

Peeps tried not to think of what might be lurking below, but he also knew that trout were nowhere to be found as long as there was an otter in the water.

As they continued to approach the flat rock on the opposite bank, Cicci began to notice something else. A large black figure, like a sentinel, was standing motionless to meet them. It was a large black bird.

"Is that...? I think it is!" Cicci focused on the landing ahead.

There, standing to greet them, was Kanti. The squirrels' spirits lifted, and they knew that their passage would now be safer.

"There Peeps, do you see?" said Cicci. "We'll all be in good... um, in good..."

"Wings?" said Peeps.

Cicci agreed, "Yes, we will be in good wings. Kanti will have more to tell us and he knows this side of the river, so he can guide us."

"Well, the sooner we are off of this barely floating bark, and safely on the bank, the better," said Peeps.

Digger had been staring into the water throughout most of the trip across and noticed something dark and large pass under their raft. He scrambled to the other side to see it pass, a bit startled when a large dark wet head emerged from the water. It was Buzz the beaver. He snorted water from his nose and greeted Digger as he chewed on a piece of bark.

"Good morning to you!"

Teek darted his attention toward the greeting. "Oh, good morning, Buzz. What a pleasant surprise."

"I thought I would add a visit to my morning work and watch you getting pulled across. This is something one does not see every cycle you know."

"For good reason," blurted Peeps.

"She is a strong swimmer, that otter. Looks like Kanti has some news for you. Mind if I listen?"

"Please do, and if you have any ideas to add, we would love to hear them."

"Quiulup! Welcome to the western bank of the river little ones." Kanti greeted them ashore.

"Kanti! Good to see you. It has been some time. You are a most welcome and pleasant surprise!" Teek exclaimed.

"I should tell you straight away that this side of the river is much different from your side."

"How so?" asked Peeps.

"Let us get you onto solid ground first. Come on, off you go."

The otter pulled the raft tight to the shore. "Well, let me see, Peeps," Kanti continued, "first, it is lit by the light of day earlier over on this side, so it gets a bit warmer, and is a bit drier, there is less cover, there are roads and ranches just over that hill…"

"What and what?" asked Peeps.

Kanti explained that roads were those long flat stretches of stone that the humans travel on, in those fast-moving beasts, for long distances at high speed.

"We know what those are. Is that what they are called? It is best to keep away from those," said Teek.

"Yes, well, you have to cross one."

"You will be there to look out for us, yes?"

"I will."

"What are ranches, Kanti?" asked Peeps.

"That is a bit more complicated to explain. They are a kind of home for the humans and the animals they care for. On our journey over the top of the rimrock, I think it will be important that you know, because that, my little friends, is our first destination. There will be a peaceful gathering of all those that speak for the different animals in our canyon. As you know this was Cicci's idea, and I must say, was the right one."

Everyone in the group turned to Cicci, who smiled and shrugged her shoulders.

Kanti continued, "I have been telling as many different creatures as I can. So has Apitah the muha, as well as To'ke-tie."

"Apitah the Muha! That's the Koosagh Diaub," added Peeps.

"Yes, Peeps, we know, now please try to keep that to yourself now. We must all be able to understand new things."

Kanti then provided more information. "During the night, in two cycles, the gathering will occur. There will be many animals from the canyon in this gathering. I will be with you to make sure you arrive safely and that you arrive when you are supposed to be there. Our journey takes us up to the top of the canyon and over the rimrock cliffs. It will be long, hot, and there is no water, so drink up now, and if you want a nibble of something, nibble now. This flat rock is a good place to refresh yourself and prepare for the journey."

The squirrels enjoyed a relaxing moment along the river with their friend Kanti. They told each other of their experiences. The squirrels told Kanti all about Ahtūn, and Kanti shared news of Apitah, To'ke-tie, Seek, and of the adventure ahead.

Kanti prepared the squirrels for what lay ahead. "There is something that I need to tell you, and this is what this gathering is all about. There are two humans that I need to talk about. Teek and I have encountered them. But I need to learn more about them between now and the gathering at night, in two cycles. I shall lead you up this cliff, then leave you and return to you in time to guide you to the gathering. At that time, I will tell you more. Now, if you are ready little ones, we can start up the hill. It has warmed up quite a bit, but if you travel from brush to boulder, I am sure that you will do just fine."

The squirrels thanked the otter, said good-bye to Buzz, picked up their satchels, and were ready for travel. Peeps watched in horror as Digger splashed river water on his face.

"What?" Digger asked.

"It is just, oh never mind." Peeps said.

"I started doing this after digging out tunnels on a hot summer day. It is very refreshing!"

"That is one word for it, I suppose."

"I will be just up the hill," said Kanti, as he lifted off.

"Must be nice to just launch into the air like that," noted Peeps.

As Kanti lifted off, he called back, "Perhaps one of these times I could carry you in my claws!"

"He doesn't miss a thing does he!"

"That is what he does, Peeps," Cicci commented.

Teek spoke. "Alright then everyone, let us get started, we have quite a climb ahead of us. Also, be very careful and stay alert. We have never been on this side of the river, and I imagine that there are still plenty of predators that do not know to leave us alone. So, stay together and take your time. There is no point in being the first to make it to the top."

"Kanti should have mentioned predators, he did not. I wonder why. He must be looking ahead," Cicci added.

The way to the top was traversed in stages and mostly without peril. Kanti was watching the whole way. The one thing he did miss was a small rattlesnake warming on a rock. It did not rattle because it noticed the squirrels first. Fortunately, the squirrels noticed him in time and moved quickly around him, and gave him plenty of room.

"There's one creature that may benefit from all of this without participating or even knowing about it," declared Peeps.

"Quiet, Peeps. He can probably hear you," Teek hissed.

Once clear of the snake, Cicci spoke. "I am noticing that this side of the river smells a little different. Does anyone else notice that?"

The breeze had picked up further up the hill, filled with the sunbaked smell of brush and minerals. There were also other smells from beyond the canyon that they could not identify. Before them now stood sheer basalt cliffs, with no obvious way up and over. Teek turned to Cicci.

"Do you see Kanti anywhere?"

"I do. He is waiting for us over by the way to the top, Teek. Do you see him over there?" She gestured with her forepaw toward the base of the cliff. There Kanti stood, preening his feathers. When they joined him, they could see the narrow way to the top. The rock cliff had split, and sandy soil had spilled down, providing a navigable trail to the top.

"See you on top!" Kanti launched himself upward once again.

"I might just take him up on that offer someday," said Peeps.

"What offer?" asked Digger.

"His offer to carry me on one of his flights."

"I am not sure that was intended as a kind offer. He did mention carrying you in his claws did he not?" asked Teek.

"I was thinking of clinging to his back."

"Well, I do not see that happening," replied Digger.

Before long the squirrels had made it up the narrow sandy pass to the top of the cliff and were circled around Kanti. At the top, one of the columns of basalt towered above, where they had gathered, providing a cool, shady spot to rest.

"Just over that hill over there, is a road, and just beyond that is a large field of grass. In the middle are three tall trees. That is where the gathering will take place. You have the end of this cycle and then until another cycle ends, so you might locate a place to hole up for the darkness. I need to find out more, possibly from other birds, but I will return soon to let you know what I find out about the fate of the canyon, and those two humans I have heard of. I *can* tell you that your next journey may very well involve a large cavern back on your side of the river, and possibly the ancient human in the burial cavern, the one you have seen. He has visited me from the spirit world. I believe that there is a power that he controls. However, I am not sure what it is or what it has to do with the two humans and the fate of this canyon. I will hopefully be able to tell you more when I return. Quiulup, kkkkkk, would you happen to have any of those flies left from your time with Ahtūn? I am a little hungry. No? Well, I can always go pick something up from the road."

"The road? What do you mean?" asked Cicci.

"Uh... nothing... I must go now." With a distinctive *fwoop-fwoop-fwoop*, he launched himself with the usual gusty scattering of sand and pebbles.

14

FAR AFIELD

"What about the ranches?" asked Peeps, as he flew off.

"I guess he will tell us about those when he returns," replied Teek. Then, glancing over at the hill, he added "How about having a peek over the hill at our destination? What do you say?"

"Quickly, then we should look for a place to hole up," Cicci answered.

"We have plenty of time, this will not take long."

They reached the top of the little hill. There they beheld a whole new world. This was the beginning of horse and cattle country where the humans lived on ranches. The squirrels peered from junipers and sagebrush at a land of open fields and few trees. Vast grasslands bordered by wooden structures for keeping large animals enclosed now stretched out before them. They were in the realm of the humans, although they could not see them. These dwellings were not close together but positioned at the end of long pathways and in the middle of vast fields.

"Look, Teek," Cicci redirected Teek's attention. He had turned around to make sure that Peeps and Digger had made it up over the edge of the cliff and out of the canyon.

Cicci, having retrieved Teek's attention, began. "There is a long slab of stone that the humans use to take journeys when they ride those large beasts, only this looks red, not black, and look over there. Another one that joins it. How do you suppose they were able to find rock so flat and smooth? Can we get closer?"

The bright light of day was directly overhead. Shadows were directly under everything. The warm wind kicked up dust and small wrappers that had been thrown by the humans passing by. They stopped above a trench that the humans had dug alongside the long flat stone surfaces. They could feel the heat radiating off the surface of the stone.

"It is a lot warmer up here above the canyon," Peeps noticed.

Teek took note of their position. "This is the place Kanti spoke of. Where one long flat stone meets another. The large grassy meeting place is just over there on the other side of this flat stone and that long wooden structure. We will have to be extra careful not to get attacked by the fast moving beasts, while crossing. The meeting will be at the end of another cycle, just under that group of three tall trees over there."

The tall trees were three old ponderosa pines in the middle of a wide field that seemed as large as an inland sea to the four ground squirrels. Teek looked over at Cicci. The warm wind whipping down the long slab of stone, parting her fir, revealing her white downy undercoat. Her nose twitched as she smelled new scents, blowing in from the other stretch of stone that met the flat red stone in front of them.

"What is that smell? This is something that I have never smelled before."

"I smell it too," said Peeps.

"So do I," said Digger.

"I think we all do," added Teek.

The sound of the rustling wind was broken by a *loud "clop, clop, clop" then ssshhclop, slap clop, clop, clop, clop.*

"Look!" squeaked Peeps.

They all looked and to their astonishment and surprise, two enormous rust-colored horses were approaching them in the middle of what we humans would understand to be a country road.

Their black withers ended in large hoofs that found it quite difficult to navigate the pavement. They clopped about slipping, stomping, and craning their necks with wide wild eyes, taking in unfamiliar territory, hoping to see something recognizable. The two horses had escaped their enclosed pasture and were now in over the heads, and way out of their element, with no ideas for returning to their pasture. They were experiencing what real freedom feels like, with all its unknowns. It had all looked so desirable on the other side of the fence. Now, they were clearly confused, weaving back and forth down the road, looking frantically for an opening in the fence, and hopelessly turning into one closed gate after another. One horse was quite put-out and upset with the other. They clomped up just feet from where the astonished adventurers were crouched.

Clop, clop, clop. "Snort, whinny, so what do we do now? Do you have any other bright ideas?" asked one horse.

Clop, clop, clop. "Well, it should be close, or was it back the other way? I cannot really tell. I have not been on this side of the fence, other than when they haul us around in that little barn-like thing... but those windows are so small."

"Oh, be quiet! So that is just great! It is just like I told you, we have no right to be here out on this road! Where does it go? You don't khtow! You said this was going to be fun! We have no water, no oats..."

The taller horse, the one with the initial idea, was beginning to realize that escaping the pasture was not such a good idea after all.

"Would you please stop complaining? I am not able to think with you carrying on like that!" he neighed, as he tried to determine which way to go.

"Well, clearly you were not thinking when you came up with this bright idea. Why start now?" continued the other horse.

There they stood in the middle of the road. The first horse, the one that had sprung the idea on the other, turned his neck around, facing back from where they had come.

"Maybe the gate is back the other way..." he wondered aloud.

"Oh terrific!" snorted the other.

"Look out! You almost ran right into it!" neighed the unwitting accomplice. A pickup whizzed by, narrowly missing the meandering horse.

"The next time you get a bright idea, keep it to yourself!"

"Stop whinnying and whining! We'll get back in."

Their heated argument, and all the whinnying and whining that went with it, trailed off behind them, until all that could be heard was the distant clop, clop, clop of hooves.

"... and I thought *we* were lost!" Peeps muttered.

"We are not lost, Peeps. I know where we are... well, we are near the meeting place. We just have to remember where we climbed up out of the canyon. Cicci, you know, right?"

"I will try. We just need to find where those two..."

"They are called roads," said Digger, who had been listening to the two horses. Although I must say, it doesn't sound as though roads are good for much."

"No, it appears that they are not," replied Teek. "What would you all prefer to do in this heat?" asked Teek. Stay in those piled-up rocks over there at the top of the cliff and wait for things to cool a bit, or head on over the to the meeting place? We could possibly find a resting place under the trees, then we'd already be there once it got dark."

Cicci spoke up. "I think that we have had about enough for today. Teek, let us crawl up under those rocks, besides Kanti should be here when we continue, and I do not think we would like to spend the rest of the bright light of day waiting in that desolate place."

The boulders had been piled up beside the road many years before. Now they were shaded by some grasses and sagebrush.

"I'm thirsty," declared Peeps.

"Nuts," said Teek. "Well then you can spend the remainder of the day climbing back down the hill to the river, and then back up. But you cannot go alone."

"I will go with him." Digger was always up for an adventure.

Teek turned to Digger and Peeps.

"I am not sure I like the idea of separating. Stay focused, and no wandering. You go straight down and straight back! Clear? Take a satchel in case you find something to eat. Look for us in that rock pile over there and call to us."

Digger and Peeps looked at each other with surprise and excitement and scampered down the hill. Sliding through the sandy shoot between the columns of rim rock cliffs, they bounded down the slope. Their first stop was halfway to the river to collect themselves under a rock that was shadowed by a large old sage, to listen, to smell, and look around. There was nothing in the sky, nothing on the surrounding rocks, and no predators out hunting at this time of day. So, with a quick reassuring glance, they headed for the flat landing rock. There, laying on the rock to their surprise was the otter, almost as though she knew they'd be there. She was chewing on the tail of a crayfish. The first thought that entered Peeps' mind was that he hoped it wasn't the crayfish that served to summon Ahtūn. To his relief, this crayfish had been much smaller.

"Welcome back," greeted the otter. "That was fast. Where are the others?"

"We just came back down for water. The others are still up at the top of the canyon. The gathering is during the darkness, in another cycle once the bright light goes down. We are usually not as far away from the river, and the climbing sort of dried us up."

With that she rolled down under the water and in just a few moments resurfaced. Inher mouth was a large bunch of wet water plants.

"Here, stuff this in your sack."

"What are these?" asked Digger.

"They hold water."

The two young squirrels thanked the otter profusely and comple-mented her on her wonderful idea, letting her know they would see her soon.

"Go save the canyon," she called back to them.

The two squirrels scampered up the hill.

"Save the canyon? Nettles!" Peeps puffed. "Does everyone know something I do not? What is that about?"

"Do not worry Peeps, the unknown is all part of this adventure. If everything were known, it would not be much of an adventure. We will find out soon enough."

"Well, I am glad someone is comfortable with that," replied Peeps.

"What I am thinking about is food!" announced Digger. "Those big flies are still all over. They are crunchy and delicious. What sayu we gather a few and throw them in the satchel?"

Peeps thought for a moment.

"We'll have to look for some seeds or nuts for Cicci. She is not too fond of flies, even though they live in the river."

"You know what Teek said about wandering out of our way. We'll gather what we can on our way back up. I am sure we will notice something."

"Yes, yes, Digger, I know what Teek said."

15

THE BEST LAID PLANS

The two humans leaned on their hands over the conference table peering down at their plans for the use and development of the canyon. Their idea of 'Land Use Planning' was their development of the habitat in the canyon. They did not consider the land to be of any good or of any 'use,' unless it was for a big profit. A false profit. In their minds, land left untouched, and water left to nature was a worthless waste, and a lost opportunity. Dennis' intentions were not in line with the well-being of the natural habitat.

What Dennis Digwood cleverly realized was that there was a large population of people who wanted the same thing, and he knew what that thing was— ownership of a 'slice of heaven.' He was the only one lucky enough to have figured out a way to get it and use it to his advantage. What Dennis failed to understand was that once everyone loved the same place, they would love it to death. Once the canyon got divided up for all of them to occupy, it would no longer be a slice of heaven. It would become a front-row seat to the destruction of nature, simply for the idea of being close to it, and owning it.

For the animals, it was their home. Trying to rebuild their destroyed dwellings on what would become human 'property' would be almost impossible. They would be considered pests, trying to live where they always had. The canyon had provided homes for the local animals and plants for thousands of years.

Dennis Digwood wanted the canyon to make him a respected and powerful pillar in the community. He was a land developer and his investor, Lucinda Musgrab, would help him get there. Dennis Digwood had lived in Central Oregon all his life. He was the son of William Digwood, a successful real estate developer. William Digwood had been a powerful and imposing force in the community. William let his son Dennis know, at an early age, that he considered him weak, and that he didn't think he would ever amount to anything if he didn't stop showing sympathy to others and wishing them well.

He'd say, "Start thinking of yourself and your future, Dennis! Nobody cares about your little 'nature fantasy' world!" In those days Dennis was kind and respectful to all the creatures in the canyon. He had told his father, whom he trusted at the time, that he had been awakened by a squirrel and so, could then understand the language of animals. He immediately discovered that his father thought him odd and foolish for thinking that animals were talking to him.

"Do not speak of this again," he said, "or I will disown you!"

Then the day came when his father made a cruel decision that broke poor Dennis' spirit. William believed that Dennis needed to be forced to change his thinking and become 'tough.' He ordered Dennis to kill all the squirrels and marmots, mice, or anything else that he had attracted to their property. He told him that they were vermin and needed to be removed. Dennis was forced to stay outside with no food and no water until such time as he had eliminated all the "vermin" from his father's property. Dennis remained outside for three days until he could stand it no more. His father had given him traps and a pellet gun for the grizzly task. Dennis was allowed inside only when all the "pests" were gone, and he was never the same person from that point on. He had been given a secret ability to understand the language of animals, and it would one day prove valuable to him in Central Oregon land development.

Dennis struggled to become a leader in the community. His father William had passed, yet his legacy remained. Dennis felt a deep need to be more successful than his father, but he still measured his success by his father's rules.

Dennis, like his father, was a large man, not fat, just big and imposing. You would think that his heart and his character would have been just as large, but it wasn't. Confidence was the number one thing that William could have instilled in Dennis, but it turned out to be the very thing that he took away from Dennis. Dennis covered his lack of confidence with nice clothes, not a suit and tie, but the sort of clothes one wears to say, "relaxing country vacation homes". His short-sleeved shirt, pleated slacks, and straw fedora presented a deceptively friendly look, but the shoes were the give-away. They were the finest leather and expensive. `   He could not keep himself from the idea of challenging others to walk a mile in his shoes, knowing full-well that many of them, couldn't afford them.

Dennis listened to his father and obeyed, keeping his hidden ability to himself and never speaking of it. Eventually, the day came when Dennis determined that it was to his personal advantage to listen in on what the animals were saying so they can exploit them and take their habitat for himself.

At that point, Dennis believed that the only thing to fill his profound emptiness was money and power. It had been drilled into him by his father that to be an adult human, you needed to be respected, powerful, own property, and be a successful land developer. Dennis now believed in the law of the jungle–eat or be eaten.

Nobody was aware that Dennis was the only human who had both the ability to know what the creatures in the canyon were saying and the hatred for what they represented–a barrier between him and what he craved more than anything– respect. He had lost his feeling for those creatures and their lives early in his life and saw his secret ability as nothing more than a way to gain an advantage over any creature that stood in his way. Nobody knew about this secret, including Teek.

"So, you can put fifty units in there? What about the rodents?" said his investor, Lucinda. She was a wealthy widow from Los Angeles. Los Angeles had created many like her. Here, along the Deschutes River she was out of her element.

"Don't worry, they'll all be gone," replied Dennis, almost talking over the top of her, then catching himself quickly.

"Good, because when these units start selling, I don't want to have to explain this to anyone, and I also want all signs of a fire, gone. Clear out all these burned trees and bushes!"

"I'll put a crew in there right away," Dennis assured.

"As soon as you arrange it, let me know. I have deadlines, and we have schedules to make up."

Cleaning up burned-out trees and brush was no problem but killing and removing all creatures from the properties would be challenging to say the least. Dennis would have to devise a plan that would stay hidden from the public. Remembering his secret ability, he began to think of how there might be a way to use the rats, use them to rid the surrounding area of squirrels, marmots, chipmunks, mice, and other rodents. Then he could poison them. They would believe that they could take over Rimrock, then all he'd have to do is kill the rats! That was easy enough. There was no law protecting them. Most people didn't even know they were there. In fact, he may even be appreciated by the local community for eliminating a rat problem. They were, after all, an invasive species!

Later, Dennis drove into the turn-around where the rats had lived in the large black pipes, the one further down the river. In his headlights, he could make out eyes reflecting the light back in his direction from the bushes. They were here. Leaving his parking lights on to cast some light on his late-night meeting, he sat on the hood of his truck and called to them.

"You rats there. I see your eyes. I will not harm you. I can tell you how to find Rimrock. I can lead you there!"

The squeaking of the rats became words Dennis could understand. What the rats could not possibly know is that everything Dennis had just said to them was a lie. He was going to try to harm them. He did not know where Rimrock was, nor how to lead them there.

Dennis heard a voice of one of the rats. "Who are you? We want to know. You are human, but you can understand us? You are not here to kill us?"

Another rat stepped out from the darkness and into the headlights. It was Eek.

"What do you want? What do you have for us? Our alpha rat, Sleg, wants to know."

"You want Rimrock. I can deliver it to you!" Dennis called out.

With those words, Eek was violently shoved out of the way to make way for the enormous Sleg. He swatted attendant rats away from his ears and neck. They had been clinging to him and screeching at him. He appeared in the car lights.

"Turn those lights down!" he screeched.

"Those are parking lights, they're as low as they go. I need them to see you."

"What is all this about Rimrock?" Sleg interrogated. "Why are you telling us? What interest is it of yours?"

"I want those squirrels gone just like you do, and I'll leave it to you to kill them and take over. I can show you where Rimrock is."

Although Dennis didn't really know where the village of Rimrock was, he knew he could get them close, and once they were close, the defending squirrels would reveal it to him. What Dennis was also not aware of was that Eek knew exactly where the village was. He was the only rat that did, but he was biding his time. He knew that Reek was the only other rat that would have known, but he had been swallowed by Ish the gopher snake who was then killed by Apitah (the young Red-tailed Hawk). Eek was the only remaining creature, outside of the Rimrock village who knew of its location. Eek had the advantage.

"Why do you want them gone, human?" Sleg continued.

Dennis did not get as far as he had gotten without knowing how to be aggressive. He quickly replied, "That, rat, is none of your business! Do you want to know where Rimrock is or not?"

"Tell us! Tell us where it is, human!"

"I will not tell you. I will show you where it is, rat! Do you know where the burned-out part of the forest is?"

"We do!"

"Meet me there in three days."

"Three days? What do you mean?"

"When the sun has appeared three times, and it is starting to disappear behind the mountains."

"Agreed. We will be there, but no tricks, human, or we will find out where you live!"

Dennis did not want the rats to know where he lived, of course, especially since it was so close, and his investor might be there in his adjoining office. His home was situated right on the rimrock cliffs above the canyon, just downriver from Rimrock.

The last thing he needed was for his home's location to become known to the creatures of the canyon.

RIMROCK AND IPSUSNUTE

"Are Teek and Kanti up there in those rocks?" Nute asked Seek.

"No, they are not." Seek replied. "First, Kanti is a friend and ally, but not a ground squirrel. He is a raven. He, and a meadowlark named To'ke-tie, bring us news, and will guide us through what may be some very difficult days ahead. Teek is a leader in our village and is away with Cicci, Peeps, and Digger. They are working with Kanti to save all our lives here in this canyon."

"There is a village?"

"Yes Nute, there is," answered Sofia. "This is what you should see next. It is a legacy left to the ground squirrels by your ancestor."

"Follow me now, Ipsusnute, and I will take you there," said Seek.

Sofia and Nute followed Seek up the hill toward the basalt cliffs, through the thick brush and found the tiny trail that led through a tangled thicket. Pushing their way through, they entered the small clearing on the other side. Seek waited to guide them through the narrow passage to the village. They watched him scurry through the narrow opening in the cliffs, the passage to the village of Rimrock. Sofia led Nute into another world, a world his own ancestor had created. A cool pungent sweetness of lush vegetation met them.

Toward the top of the narrow cliffs were old pine trees, junipers, and sagebrush, sending roots down into the moist cracks, where subterranean springs of cold fresh water streamed down the smooth walls of stone, dribbled, and dripped enough to nourish them. Their old roots wound tightly around the basalt and bore deeply into the moist cracks. The pair continued following Seek through the curvy narrow passage sliding by beautifully colorful clumps of wildflowers and splashes of orange and yellow lichen. Tiny birds would flit and dart from their hiding places as they passed, and bright blue lizards flitted across the rocks.

"It is as if time has stood still in this place," Sofia commented quietly.

"It very well may have," answered Nute.

Sofia stopped and stared at Nute for a few seconds, realizing for the first time that there was more to this magical place than the natural world. Seek vanished around a bend, and Sofia grabbed Nute and pulled him forward. He looked up wondering where the passage might be positioned from above. He could see the thin sliver of blue sky and some flittering yellow butterflies passing from one wall to the other. They passed a cavernous opening and could hear a deep rumbling that sounded very much like breathing, yet much deeper and much louder.

"I hear that you need to keep moving and never stop there, Nute," said Sofia, as she motioned him to keep moving. He followed without a word.

"This place is not part of the rest of the canyon, Sofia. It is not part of this world." It exists here and is being shown to us now, but we would not be able to find this otherwise," observed Nute.

"You know this?"

"Somehow, I do."

"This way!" Seek had returned to them. "Keep moving," he urged.

After some time, Seek, Sofia, and Nute arrived at the entrance to Rimrock, which lay in a tiny round bowl-shaped valley at the bottom of enclosed basalt cliffs. Nute stood speechless as he took in the view. Sofia stood staring at his face, then staring back at the village. It had been some time since she had stood before this magical land, a hidden valley of boulders, green grassy areas, gardens, clear pools, and clear tiny creeks, the source of which were rivulets of water running down the cliff faces. Between the boulders, sandy soil, and gardens, were tiny houses, walkways, and doors. There were ground squirrels scampering this way and that, occasionally stopping to stare in that familiar frozen way of ground squirrels. The villagers had all been warned about the visiting humans, and some of them had been told of the young Ipsusnute, the descendant of the ancient one that they had learned of in storytelling time at Colony Hall. They stared at Nute as though seeing a vision of Ipsusnute himself. In fact, Sofia and Nute could hear an occasional whisper of "Ipsusnute."

"You may sit in the middle of that grassy area in front of Rimrock Creek. Watch your step though as you enter the village, we have some spearheads to defend against intruders, along with the guards that you will notice to your left and right. They sound off in case there is a breach of the barrier."

Sofia and Nute took their positions carefully, sitting cross-legged on the grass in front of the creek. They were conscious not to disturb the crisscrossing trails, although they had to sit on them. The two of them filled most of the grassy area, but they both sat perfectly still because they knew that having large humans in the middle of the village was still a bit intimidating, no matter who they were. All around them, ground squirrel villagers sat on porches, peered from doorways, from gardens, on or behind boulders, and next to the creek, to behold and overhear. All attention was focused on the humans. Some were a little fearful; others crept boldly closer.

"Everything is so fresh and lush here. Does it stay this way all through summer?" Sofia wondered aloud.

"I think it does. I imagine that he makes sure it stays that way."

"But not when it gets cold and the snow starts," said Seek. "That is when everything sleeps."

"How little the humans know. Most humans passing by don't even know that Rimrock exists. This is like an isolated, enchanted Eden," Sofia whispered softly.

Seek stood before them, the only ground squirrel on their side of the creek.

"This, as I am sure you know by now, is Rimrock, our hidden village, our home. Not since the stealing of our Illumination Stone had we worried about our future and our fate. Now, all that has changed. The theft of the Illumination Stone and the arrival of the rats in the canyon were only the beginning." He sighed. "Now we face a much greater threat. The entire canyon is in peril. This threat is not natural, it is the encroachment on our world by humans, the rats are only one part of this occupation.

Seek paused and then said, "Kanti has told me that he and Teek's party are exploring ways to defend the canyon from the destruction of our homes and our world, by humans. But we also hear that the rats are looking to take over Rimrock. Once they find it, we are all in great danger. I fear that we must ask for help from humans once again."

"Seek, it would be better if we were able to get some idea of when this is all happening."

"Yes, Sofia, I agree. That is why I sent word with To'ke-tie back to Kanti.

"Who is To'ke-tie?" asked Nute.

"He is what you humans would refer to as a Western meadowlark."

"How wonderful, a western meadowlark is a messenger!" Nute marveled. This was a world he had always known in his heart was real, but rarely had seen any evidence of it.

Seek continued. "If Kanti and the Koosagh Diaubs..."

"Those what?" asked Nute.

"Red-tailed hawks. Koosagh Diaub is what the ground squirrels call them," added Sofia.

"Oh."

Nute began to think about how some of this could start to make sense. "If Kanti and 'the hawks' can listen closely and follow their activity, they can help us understand their plan. To'ke-tie is expected back tomorrow morning."

"I can stay here tonight. Sofia, you leave me here and return tomorrow morning. Okay?"

"I want to stay too!"

"I think it'd be best if you didn't. My family expects that behavior of me from time to time."

"Yeah, well I expect that of my mom too, but she didn't come home last night!"

"Her name is Helen, right?" asked Seek. "She is Walter's offspring?"

"Yes."

"So, you are her kit?"

"You could say that."

"How is dear Walter? Where is he?"

"I shall bring him to you soon."

Nute spoke up. "It is all about trust, isn't it? You need to know what to expect from someone?"

"My mom is more about 'Do as I say, not as I do'."

"Well, do what you think is right, Sofia. Set a good example. I'll be fine down here. I'm used to it. I sleep on the ground all the time."

"You do? Where?"

"In places like this. You know, out away from everything."

"He can sleep in our passage, that is a safe and secure spot," mentioned Seek.

"What about food and water?"

"The best water in the canyon is right here, and maybe they'll bring me some nuts and berries."

"Done!" said Seek. "Dried grasshoppers?"

"Uh, no thank you. No bugs for me. Nuts and berries are just fine," Nute replied. "Sofia, I have a good feeling about staying down here. You go now, I'll be right here when you return in the morning."

"I know, I just don't want to miss anything."

"You won't. We'll wait for you. You're in charge, you know."

"All right then, if I'm in charge, we need your coat and a blanket!"

"I have those right here in my backpack"

"Okay, I'll go and come back in the morning then."

Nute followed Sofia back up the hill and watched her ride away. He hiked back down the hill. Seek showed him a good spot with soft sandy soil to lay on in the passage. As he lay there he thought, *She sure doesn't waste any time, I bet she's back bright and early.*

"Nute! Wake up!"

"Huh? Oh, Sofia! Good morning."

"Recovering from the nuts and berries, are we? You didn't sleep very well, did you?"

"I guess not. It was a bit colder than I thought it'd be."

"I knew it! if you hadn't had your coat and a blanket, you'd have frozen!"

"What time is it?"

"Seven."

"Seven! No wonder!"

"What did you expect?"

"Eight."

"Don't be silly! I've already peeked into the village, and they are waiting for us. To'ke-tie has not arrived yet but Seek expects him soon. C'mon!"

Nute put his coat on, rolled up the blanket, and followed Sofia to the village.

"There you are. You are welcome to some spring water, if that helps."

"Do you have any coffee?" Nute muttered.

"Sorry? I did not hear that," replied Seek.

"Nothing. Water is great."

"You drink coffee?" Sofia was surprised.

"Occasionally, when I haven't slept well."

"To'ke-tie should be here soon," said Seek. "We will know more then. Once we know the rats' plan of attack, we should be able to formulate our own plan for defense."

A young squirrel serving as an assistant scrambled up with news. "Master Seek, To'ke-tie has just arrived, he has landed outside the doors of Colony Hall and is waiting for you."

"Ah yes, I see him."

Seek waved To'ke-tie over, assuring him that the two humans were not a threat.

"Greetings To'ke-tie. Is everyone well and safe?"

"All are well, and on their way,
to the land of grass and horses.
Humans send rats to ruin all
and gather up their forces."

"I am afraid that To'ke-tie's message is going to require a little interpretation," concluded Seek.

Sofia thought for a moment and then suggested that Seek try asking a specific question.

"Maybe you should ask him if Kanti mentioned when he thinks that the rats will reach Rimrock."

Seek asked that very question of To'ke-tie, and the bird's answer was:

"The rats are on their way,
Three cycles from today,
but you need have little fear,
for birds of prey are near,
and in the walls of Rimrock,
two good humans stay!"

"Kanti knows of our whereabouts?" asked Nute.

"Yes, Nute. Kanti knows just about everything that is going on in the canyon. Kanti has also started using other birds, like the songbirds, as messengers. Birds are everywhere. They hear everything. This one, To'ke-tie, has specifically been sent to report the movements and location of Teek's group. But the rats heading for Rimrock also involve Teek, so he reports on that too. This is an ever-changing situation."

"I think that in this situation, we should return each day to check on your village," suggested Sofia.

"I want to meet Kanti the raven. He might be an ancestor of mine too." Nute had grown up with the notion that spirits can take animal form.

"He would possibly have mentioned something about that, would he not?" inserted Seek. "You should find Kanti before the rats come.

He can tell you where to position yourself. You see, according to To'ke-
tie here…"

"He flew away," Sofia said, still watching him go.

"What? He… Oh well, that was probably all he had to tell us. I
wanted him to report to Kanti that you are here. You need to know if
you are to be outside or inside the village. You may very well be inside
since the Koosagh Diaubs and other predators will no doubt be outside
of our walls. Will Kanti be here ahead of them?"

"We have time," replied Sofia. "To'ke-tie mentioned 'Two good
humans' in his song. Tomorrow we will hike downriver and see if we
can find him, and we'll bring Walter." Sofia and Nute rose and headed
back toward the passage. Nute looked back to get another look at the
village, smiled at Seek, and shook his head once.

"You tell Walter that we miss him and want to see him soon," Seek
called out.

"We will. You will see him sooner than you think!" Nute replied.

Sofia and Nute walked out through the passage. Sofia spoke first.
"If there were an easier way down here, my grandpa would want to be
here."

"There is."

"What?"

"There is an easier way down here."

"Where?"

"Where the fire was."

"How do you know?"

"Oh, I've been here before."

Sofia shoved him again. "Why didn't you tell me?"

"There are hardly any places I haven't been down here, well, not
Rimrock, but many places. I keep mostly to the main trail. There's a
dirt road in that burned out turn-around now. They took out the
burned trees and brush. Then there are two trails that head down the
slope to the river, one goes upriver, and one goes down. Neither one of
them are very steep. Then we just help him upriver a short distance to
Rimrock. It will be challenging, but it is important."

Sofia stared at him, then finally agreed. The two walked back up
the hill.

17

THE GATHERING

"Teek! Teek!"

"Down here!"

Peeps and Digger followed Teek's call to a rather small opening in the pile of boulders. Once inside, it opened into a larger, hollowed-out chamber.

"How did it go?" Teek asked. "You are back sooner than I thought you would be."

"That otter met us at the landing rock. She gave us some wet water plants to put in one of the satchels. Is anyone thirsty?" Peeps asked, as he held up the satchel containing the plants.

Teek and Cicci looked at each other in puzzlement, but after all was explained, they filled their cheeks with the plants and found them to be cool and refreshing.

"In the other satchel, we have gathered a few of those flies."

Cicci opened her eyes wide and glanced at Teek.

"Anything else?" she asked quietly and hopefully.

"There is! Thanks to Peeps' thinking, we also have some seeds and nuts for you."

Peeps was most appreciative of Digger's comments and the credit given to him. They were becoming fast friends.

"Why, thank you for thinking of me Peeps," Cicci acknowledged.

"There is something else. As we reached the top of the cliff, Digger found this bag, half full of these flat crunchy things. They must have been thrown from the road. Can we try some?"

"Let me see one." Teek examined it carefully. "I have tried these before, they made me very thirsty. Go ahead and taste it but do not have too much. Cicci how about you?"

"Well, maybe just one, for taste," she said quietly.

Soon, the bag was empty.

"I am enjoying this adventure," declared Digger.

"I guess at the moment, I am too," admitted Peeps, "but everyone keeps mentioning how perilous our adventure will be and how we are supposed to save the canyon. It makes me quite nervous."

"All we can do is our best, and make the best decisions we can, when the time comes." Teek's message comforted those around him. "It is also good to remember the lessons we learned from our last adventure about this community of creatures all working together. We have help, Peeps. That's what this gathering is about."

Peeps shoulders relaxed.

"Yes, well that is another thing. What are all these creatures that will be in this gathering? There will be predators among them, right?"

"Yes, there will be, Peeps, but they have all taken a vow not to attack any creature in the gathering. We all want the same thing, to save our canyon," Teek maintained a reassuring tone. "Kanti and other birds, like the Muhas, have called this gathering. If you remember, he has saved us more than once. Now get some rest. When the bright light of day arrives, we will have much to do."

"We will? I wish I knew what it was!"

"We all do, Peeps."

⚬━━◈◆◈━━⚬

Teek began to prepare everyone for their next task. "Now remember, these large, brightly colored beasts that carry the humans along this flat stone? They move very fast. So, we want to make sure that there are none in sight. This is not about beating them. They would be on you before you knew it. I am not completely sure if it is better that we all go at once, or one at a time."

"This is worse than a deep fast river!" replied Peeps.

"It is like that kind of danger, Peeps. I wish Kanti were here," Teek added, "he could keep a lookout."

"I am." There was Kanti, perched on a rock directly behind them.

"Bristles! Do you have to do that every time?" exclaimed Peeps.

"It is what I do."

"I sort of agree with Peeps, Kanti," Teek commented. "You could have said something or called to us before you landed. This is no place to be surprised."

"If I fly over this road and make sure that there is nothing heading this way, you should be able to all go at once. That would be best. Can I grab a satchel or two?" With that, he grabbed the satchels and launched himself. Flying above them, he called out, "All clear! Ready? Go!"

The squirrels scrambled across the hot road to the other side and into the tall grass in the ditch on the outside of the wooden fence that bordered the vast pastureland.

"Nicely done! Are you in there somewhere, little ones?" Kanti called into the ditch with a chuckle. "I must say that was quite a sight."

"I am so glad we could amuse you," replied Peeps.

"Crawl under this wooden barrier, and I will meet you on the other side. Then we can head over to those tall trees out in the middle, and I can tell you what I have learned."

Once on the other side of the wooden planks, they peered out across what looked like an endless sea of golden waving grass. Kanti was perched on a wooden post above them.

"Well, what do you think? Are you ready?"

"As we shall ever be," replied Teek.

The trek across the pastureland seemed to go on forever, partly because the grass was way over their heads, so that all they could really see, other than the light golden stalks of grass that they pushed through, was straight up. Kanti was always in sight, either flapping his wings to hover above them or soaring in circles around them. The crunching and rustling under their scrambling paws were the only sounds for some time.

They reached a point that felt as though they may not be able to continue. They were just about ready to give up when Cicci happened to look up again.

"Look, everyone," she gasped for air as she spoke. "We find refuge under his wings!"

"What is that you say?" asked Teek.

"I do not know. It just came to me."

They all looked up again and noticed that Kanti was no longer soaring alone. There were several hawks and even some golden eagles soaring in circles with him.

The air was hot and dry, the cool spicy fresh air of the canyon had been replaced by a stifling grassy heaviness. Still, they pressed on, spirits now lifted by the site of those impressive birds.

"I can hardly breathe! I feel like I am drowning!"

"Keep going, Peeps. We must be almost there. Look! Do you see? The trees are just ahead."

"They are still quite a distance away. They just look closer because they are so big!"

"Hang in there, Peeps."

"Ah, finally, that is better," declared Cicci.

This immediately captured Teek's attention. "What is better, Cicci? How are you? Do you want to stop?"

"Do you not notice? The bright light of day is no longer beating down on us. We are in the shade of the three tall trees!"

"So, we are! Look Peeps! Look Digger! We are in the shadow of the tall trees. They are right above us! If we head over to their trunks, it should be a nice, protected spot."

As they approached the nearest tree, they could see Kanti perched on a lower dead branch waiting for them.

"That was not so terribly bad, was it?"

"Well, we could not fly here, but we made it," replied Peeps.

"I think you will find that it was worth it. There will be many animals here when the bright light descends and darkness falls, united once again after a very long time, and it is for good reason."

Peeps glanced at Digger, then addressed Kanti. "Perhaps on the way back I can ride on your back."

"I was thinking more of my claws, or talons. I am sure my friends would agree with me, but we will see."

Kanti lifted his beak upwards to acknowledge the group he had guided there. Way up, in the uppermost branches of the tall pines perched several large hawks and eagles, one of which was Apitah. Peeps gulped and remained silent for most of the rest of the night.

"Kanti," Teek began, "Once we have a chance to rest for a little while, get some water from the river weeds, and some nibbles, can you tell us more?"

Kanti hopped down from the branch. Using his wide wings to slow his descent, he glided down to them. "I will tell you more. There are some important developments, they may change things for you a bit, but I also have some information about the journey ahead of you, which I am certain that you will welcome."

The group spent the remainder of the heat of the day resting under the cool canopy of the pines, sipping from the river weeds, and crunching on bugs, nuts, and seeds.

Kanti had tucked his head under one wing, leaving one eye above, to instantly open upon hearing the slightest disturbance.

Finally, Teek approached Kanti. "We are ready to hear of the happenings now, Kanti."

All the squirrels gathered around Kanti and focused their attention on him.

"Alright, here it is. This canyon is highly desired by the humans. They all want the same thing: your homes. Right now, our biggest enemy is a human named Dennis Digwood."

"Always pay attention to names," added Peeps. "Always."

"He intends to rid his development in the canyon of all rodents. That includes you. He is directing the rats toward Rimrock, so we need to refocus our attention now on defending your home. This gathering is important for the canyon, but if Rimrock falls, it is a major setback for all of us. Your next journey is back to Rimrock to defend your village."

"Kanti, are you saying that once this gathering is over, we must return to Rimrock?"

"Yes."

The bright light of day eventually dropped down behind the Cascades, and there was darkness. Most of the animals in the canyon were represented in the gathering. From beavers to badgers and from otters to osprey, all came to listen. There were deer, elk, various cats, coyotes, bears, badgers, martens, minks, mallards, geese, raccoons, chipmunks, and squirrels of all varieties, all the way down to mice, lizards, and snakes. There was also a marmot by the name of Wuchak. The rats were the only animals not represented, of course, but most everything else, from beavers to badgers and from otters to osprey, all came to listen. There were deer, elk, various cats, coyotes, bears, martins, minks, mallards, geese, raccoons, chipmunks, and squirrels of all kinds, all the way down to mice, lizards, and snakes. There was also a marmot by the name of Wuchak. Two quarter horses, who just happened to find their way back to the safer side of the fence, stood and nervously watched in amazement, wondering how all those different animals had come to show up in their pasture.

There were also many birds perched in the pine trees. Thousands of them filled the branches above. So much so that their calls created a ruckus so loud, it was making it difficult to hear anything that was being said. There were owls, thrushes, finches, various corvids, robins, blackbirds, thrushes, and so on. There were even hummingbirds that relentlessly chased each other from limb to limb. There was also a very special and important bird, a western meadowlark.

Kanti, situated in the center of the large circle of animals, held up his wings to silence the gathering and call them to order.

"Remember," he said, "we must not call attention to ourselves, and to this gathering. There are animals here that must remain hidden and undetected simply to be able to survive, so please respect them. It is also important that everyone be able to hear what is being said. Please settle down and be silent."

As silence fell on the gathering, it was soon broken by heavy foot-falls, and the snapping of large branches that had broken off and fallen to the ground.

"That sounds like two legs... a human!" Digger's voice cut through the group of animals around him, causing them to chatter to one another and look around nervously.

"That is no human," Teek corrected. "Do you smell that?"

"I most certainly do. It is horrid!"

"Do not say that loudly, Peeps!" ordered Teek. "Without pointing, look over behind the trees and tell me what you see."

"Two large eyes brightly shining back at me, but they are way too high off of the ground to be standing there."

"Are you sure about that?"

"You are not serious."

"I am."

"What is it?"

"There are two of them."

Teek continued to stare toward the center of the gathering circle as he spoke. He had been told not to call attention to them. Peeps knew what Teek was referring to from their last journey but was still silenced by Kanti's earlier warnings and so, said nothing.

"All right, what are they?" asked Digger, "I can hear them breathing all the way over here."

"If you think that is loud, just wait until you hear their call."

"Teek, what are they? How do you know?"

Teek continued staring out into the center of the gathering "They are called, among other things, "sasq'ets," or "hairy man." The humans around here call them sasquatch, or worse yet, bigfoot. They are much larger than a bear and are by far the most elusive creature here. Understandable, as they are the most sought-for creatures on the planet by humans. Kanti was made aware of them and so he needed to know what they were, of course, so he found out from other birds, and then, well, he told me. This creature is very important to us because this territory is very important to *them*. Believe it or not, native humans consider them to be guardians of our world, but you must never ever approach one. They are very fast and will eat you, well maybe not tonight, but usually they are difficult to escape from. But please understand, this night is different, so for now there is no need to worry. Every creature here is here to help. I have a feeling that they will show up when they are most needed, and in just the right place."

"Yes, well, there is something very unnerving about them, Teek."

"I should think so."

Digger and Peeps continued to stare at the space between the trees, at the shining eyes.

"They are very strange. I remember that night at Tibb's Burrow."

"Yes, but Peeps, right now, it is best to ignore them."

"They're moving from side to side. If I were closer, or if my back were to them, like those coyotes over there, well, I'm not sure I could..."

"Peeps! Kanti is about to speak to the gathering!"

Kanti was positioned in the middle of the circle of animals and addressed them. "Creatures of Deschutes Canyon, we welcome you all. We have gathered you here so that you may know that your canyon needs your help. First, I want to tell you that there is a ground squirrel in this gathering. His name is Teek."

His eyes scanned the crowd until they found the squirrel.

"Teek, would you step forward so that everyone can see you?"

He did as he was asked, and stood beside Kanti.

"This is Teek everyone. He and those with him are from the village of Rimrock. They are ground squirrels. You may know that already. The ancient human has chosen Teek and those close to him, to lead this effort... they are able to access places that the rest of you cannot, above ground and below, they are also quite stout-hearted and have been with the ancient one. They are very important to all of us, so we ask that you not hurt them or be troublesome to them in any way. Teek, do you have anything to say?"

Teek now spoke from a place beyond his own mind. It was as though there was a voice speaking through him. "All of us must now set aside the way of wild things. I know this will be difficult, and for those who are not with us now, it might be impossible. You can find nourishment, but it might be different than you are used to for a while. Seek each other's help. We must help each other survive. This is easier for a prey animal to say than it is for a predator. We know this to be true. That is why, for now, we must help each other. We must all defend our right to live here together in this canyon."

Kanti continued. "You may, or may not know what we all now face, so I will tell you as clearly as I can. We must all come together and try to do whatever creatures of your kind *can* do. This will be different for each of you, but your challenge is for the same purpose. The humans and the rats that they brought here are trying to take our homes from us. You know of this and where it is happening. The humans will be the most destructive to our habitat. This human of which I speak will be using the rats to try to destroy us. The rats are advancing on the village of Rimrock. We must not let Rimrock fall. We must all do what we can and work together to defend ourselves. Some of you may be better at handling the rats, others might be better at handling humans. I, and those like me, might be better at gathering information and reporting to you. Go back to your habitat and others of your kind. Figure out what you can do to help. This is when we must now all help each other to protect our homes."

Kanti then stopped and stood motionless, listening. The cool air of darkness and all the creatures remained quite still, but then a warm wind picked up. It swept in a circle around the gathering, picking up speed, it brought with it an ancient smell; air from eons past, way back from the time when creatures and humans spoke to each other. Although it was not anything the creatures had smelled before, it was somehow familiar to them. The creatures looked at each other as if they were seeing the other creatures for the first time, not with hunger or instinct, but with a common understanding. The circle of creatures stepped back as the wind continued circling. As it did, it lifted Kanti off the ground. Above him, and in the center of the gathering, floating in the air, a mist formed. It spun quickly. At first, it was formless, but soon it began to condense, it spun faster and began to take on a shape. Every animal in that gathering knew what they beheld. It was the Ancient One, Ipsus-nute. They were all motionless, their gazes fixed as a bright light radiated out from the glowing figure, in all directions, striking their faces. As if awakening them to the truth, they became united to a new reality. They knew that they were all one. They were the same. Hunger– satisfied, fear– dissolved. As suddenly as they had appeared, the radiating beams withdrew quickly into a single point of light several feet above Kanti's head and disappeared. For some time, the creatures all crouched in silence, in complete darkness. As their eyes adjusted, the cool light of night became brighter in the sky, stars began to twinkle, and they were each illuminated once more, understanding each other and their world.

"Oh, my," said Peeps. "I, I, is that what it was like that time in the burial chamber, Teek?"

"Yes, that was the Ancient One, Peeps. Remember when you found the passageway of the burial chamber?"

"To be honest, I was just trying to find a way out of there. I will say though, that I am noticing that I am no longer as afraid of the other animals."

"And for now, there is no reason to be," replied Teek. "There are times like these that we all need to help each other survive."

Kanti spoke. "All of you, go back to your kind. You know what is best for you, and how you can help. You now know what the ancient one wants you to know."

With two beats of his wings, he floated over to the small group of squirrels. "You all stay here tonight, under the pines. We will start back when the bright light first appears."

"But Kanti, those large scary, dark..."

"Don't worry, Peeps. They are gone now."

Just then To'ke-tie landed in front of Kanti.

"To'ke-tie, do you bring a message?"

Two good humans
with Seek at Rimrock
Walter Prudy
stays within, so
follow me, follow me
to the Pine Stone Inn

"It seems, little ones, that I must start back now."

Kanti hopped over to Teek and spoke directly to him.

"I shall fly to the Pine Stone Inn. There, when the bright light of day appears, I shall finally meet Walter Prudy, his granddaughter Sofia, and the descendant of Ipsusnute!" Looking back, Kanti spoke to Peeps, "Your chance to fly will have to wait."

Peeps was still a little uneasy, saying quietly, "I had hoped you had forgotten. It was just an idle thought."

"I do not forget." He stared down his long beak at Peeps, then he spoke to Teek. "Teek, I imagine that you will be seeing Walter Prudy soon. But please do not allow your excitement to take your attention away from your journey back. Be extra cautious. The rats are advancing. Travel directly to Rimrock."

18

MUSTERING FORCES

"Is everything on schedule?" Dennis asked, as he headed toward the door.

"Everything is as planned," answered Bill, his assistant. "How are you ridding the area of all those squirrels?" Bill was not on Dennis' page. Not many were.

"You mean the rodent problem? You leave that up to me. That is not your job, they will be taken care of. I know what I'm doing. Soon, everything will be taken care of, Bill! Come with me, we are going to the site."

"But, sir, it is nearly..."

"NOW! Bring the truck around! Do you want a job? Ricky is meeting us there. Him I can depend on. Remind me, what do I keep you around for?"

"Common sense?"

"What was that?"

"Constant expense?"

"Yes! Well, not for long! If it weren't for your sister..."

Bill's sister Trisha had married Dennis, for better or for worse. She was starting to realize what 'worse' was like. Bill had become used to being threatened each time he was asked to drop everything and obey.

"Drive!"

They drove toward Dennis' development on the rimrock above the river. To get there, they had to drive through an older neighborhood. One that had previously been the closest to the canyon. Dennis had turned the end of their street into an entrance to his development that would limit the current residents the ability to take a quiet hike through the woods and down to the river.

The elderly Mrs. Ainsley lived in the last house on the left before his development. Dennis spotted her in the front flower bed on her hands and knees.

"Pull over here!" he ordered.

Dennis knew he needed to keep Mrs. Ainsley on *his* side. Dennis' real estate development had been partly her land and partly government land. Mrs. Ainsley was largely responsible for testifying for him in the city council meetings and helping him acquire it and develop it.

In desperation, Gladys agreed to his deal because she needed the money to stay in her family home. Now, she was beginning to see what he really was and began to realize that no price was worth what was about to happen, but it was too late.

"Mrs. Ainsley! How are you dear?"

"What is going on today, Dennis?"

"Nothing you need worry about. Just taking care of a few details."

"You know, I've been thinking..."

"Well, you just keep that up! Say, I'm pretty late, in a frightful hurry. If you'll excuse me, I have to keep moving." With a smile on his face and a sharp kick for Bill's shin, he pulled himself back from the passenger window and they sped off.

Mrs. Ainsley was left standing, waving the dust out of her face, and shaking her head in frustration. She lowered her head and stared at the ground with deep regret.

"Too late for her, thank you very much!" Dennis snickered, the instant he was out of earshot. "There's Ricky! Let me out! I'll ride back with him. Hey Ricky!"

"Mr. Digwood! After you!"

Dennis made no contact or show of appreciation, he just kept right on walking past Ricky and toward the ledge. Ricky Harvey was young, aggressive, and a recent transplant from Atlanta. It was a major decision, and a difficult one for his young family to make, but he had visited Central Oregon and felt that it was a good place for his family. He knew he'd have to pay the price working for Dennis, but he had worked for difficult people before, he knew how to survive.

"You stay here! I'll be right back."

"I'll need you more after the rats have killed the squirrels. When it comes time to kill the rats!"

"Yessir, Mr. Digwood."

"You got that right, Ricky!"

Dennis didn't want Ricky, or any other human, to know about his secret ability to communicate with animals. He dropped down off the side of the turn-around and called to the rats.

"You rats! Digwood here!"

Eek emerged from under a rock. "Tell us human, is it time?"

"Nearly."

"We move out at dusk."

"I'll be at the next location, just upriver. I'll park the truck near a large pile of boulders just in the burned area at the top of the hill."

Neither Digwood nor the rats knew at the time, that this was also the location of Wuchak's Pine Stone Inn.

"That is where you, and the rest of your pack, can hole-up for the night."

Eek bared his yellow teeth with eager anticipation. "I will go give Sleg the good news!"

Ricky was waiting in the truck. "Did you find them?"

"I found them."

"How are you going to get the rats there? Hell, *I* don't even know where to go."

"You leave that part to me. Now drive to the next site upriver!"

"Yessir, Mr. Digwood."

The dust and gravel kicked up as they sped off.

⸺⸻◆⸺◆⸺◆⸻⸺

Walter awoke in his big comfortable chair, to the familiar knock on his door. He grabbed his cane and walked slowly to answer. He opened the door to Sofia and Nute.

"Oh, Grandpa, you should be sitting down for this."

Once all seated, Sofia began to describe the situation in the canyon, at Rimrock, and the approaching rats, and a raven named Kanti. Then Nute added some words to let Walter know about the new land development near Rimrock, and that their hope was that they could get him down there the following day.

"Yes, yes, I must go, I must be with the Rimrock squirrels."

"May we stay here with you tonight, Grandpa? I can take the spare bedroom and Nute can sleep on the couch... and... could you call mom and tell her?"

"I will. I think I know just what to say, you taught me well."

"You mustn't lie, remember?"

"I don't need to. I *do* need some extra help this evening, Sofie, so that is no lie. I need your help preparing for tomorrow. She doesn't need to know about tomorrow or Nute for that matter. I'll go call her now."

He returned from the kitchen sooner than they had expected.

"Did you talk to her?"

"Well, no. She didn't answer. I will call her later. We have plenty of time for that."

Walter took a seat in his big comfy chair.

"I have been reading the papers and noticing the local news. Who is this Dennis Digwood fellow? It seems he has been trying to develop areas around the canyon."

"I don't know about him, Grandpa. Is he the one who has been bulldozing up the forest just above the rimrock? Do you have the newspaper? Can we read it?"

"Over there on that stack by the fire. It's not surprising that you don't know. Bring it here. I noticed that the story was sort of buried in the back of the paper. I'm guessing that he has convinced the press not to give it a lot of attention. People up to no good, particularly when it involves money, don't want to draw a lot of attention to themselves."

"Yes, I've noticed that too," added Nute.

"Ah, here's where the article starts... second to the last page."

Folding it open, he pointed to the small headline. *A New Development along the Deschutes River.*

"There. It starts on this page. I seem to remember a man by the name of Digwood some years ago. If it is the same Digwood, this one learned from the worst kind of human."

Sofia and Nute sat side by side and read the article, occasionally stopping to look at each other, as they made connections and put more of the story together.

"This explains a lot. We should bring this paper with us," said Sofia.

The three spent a quiet evening answering Walter's many questions and listening to his advice while packing food and soda for the following day.

The next morning Sofia an Nute helped Walter to his pickup and left early for the canyon. Walter insisted on driving, Sofia sat in the middle, and Nute next to the window with his elbow hanging out. He loved breathing in the morning air in Central Oregon. Soon they arrived at the turnout for the canyon.

The dirt road had dug through a juniper forest on the way to the edge of the rimrock. They passed a herd of seven white-tailed deer, flicking their ears and tails as they foraged in a field.

Walter felt compelled to express his feelings. "It's a wonder Dennis doesn't want to kill them too. I guess they sort of symbolize the pretty woodland neighborhood. 'We want to let some in but not others.' Sound familiar Nute?"

"Grandpa, I don't suppose you could just enjoy seeing some deer, could you?"

"Well, I don't like the idea of him encroaching on this habitat and possibly ruining it! This place has been special. It wasn't created for the benefit of Dennis Digwood." He then glanced over at Nute and Sofia with anger in his eyes.

They pulled up to a truck already parked in the turn-around, soon to be a cul-de-sac. Dennis was craning his neck around the cab to see who had the nerve to approach them.

"Hey, you!" Dennis called out sharply, "You can't park there! This is private property!"

"I saw no signs posted." Walter leveled his gaze at Dennis.

Dennis seemed to understand that Walter was not to be trifled with.

"Besides I have been coming here all my life. You would not deny an old man of one last look, would you?"

Ricky spoke up, compelled by Walter's reasonable request. "I suppose we could..."

Dennis interrupted Ricky before he could finish, saying, "Shut up! Go back to the truck!" Dennis sized up Walter with his eyes in an attempt to gather more information. Then finally he said, "You get ten minutes, then I want you out of here!"

"It sounds to me that we should go now."

"That's a good idea, old man!"

"But Grandpa!"

Walter turned his back on Dennis Digwood, glanced quickly at Sofia, closed his eyes, and shook his head slightly, letting her know that she was to leave right away, without saying another word.

The three climbed back into the truck and backed up. Walter then explained it all to them.

"I know another little hidden pullout. If he believes that we're truly leaving, he will never think to look, and there is plenty of cover in this little pullout that will make the truck difficult to see. It's just a short distance from here. If we're careful, we can hit the trail upriver to Rimrock undetected."

"As long as this Digwood fellow thinks I'm really leaving, we can avoid a lot of trouble, at least for now. I'll turn in right here!"

"Here? But..."

"This is the spot!"

Walter pulled the pickup into an overgrown clearing. They drove over some brush and small seedlings, but it was all quite low and open for parking a vehicle. Walter's pickup was a dark grey and now was surrounded by thick tree cover and so, if seen through the trees, would have appeared as nothing more than a large boulder.

Walter pointed to a boulder. "This is a very old spot. Few people know about it."

"The hike ahead isn't easy, Grandpa."

"I'll be fine, knowing that I'm seeing Rimrock again will keep me going."

"As long as you're going to be careful. I know you want to see your friends, Grandpa, and I know this is frustrating for you, but we want to help you get there. You are quite valuable to us, so let us help you make sure that you're safe."

They walked to the edge of the clearing where a narrow trail dropped down off to the left, between rocks and through trunks of ponderosa pines. Long golden needles covered the ground. It was clear to both Sofia and Nute that no one had passed this way in a long while.

"Okay, Grandpa, here we go."

Nute stood close to him and held him steady. Walter also used his cane.

A croaking sort of voice then came from a branch in one of the trees.

"Walter? Walter Prudy? Kkkkkk!"

Sofia and Nute looked at Walter. He was staring up into the trees. There, perched on a low branch was Kanti.

"Walter Prudy? Is that you?"

"Yes, I am Walter Prudy. Who are you?"

"I am Kanti, a raven."

"I have heard of you. You are the eyes of the forest. You have guided and guarded our dear friends. I should have met you before now. You tell me, and us, what we need to do, and we will do it!"

"First, thank you, Walter Prudy. I have heard so much about you as well. You came back to your home and want to save it. You are an honored in this canyon."

"I am only a guest, and with my remaining years, will remain a guest. As all humans should be."

Kanti sat on the branch for a while, as if to think of Walter's words, then addressed Walter again. "Teek speaks of you. I am grateful for your help, we here in the canyon need it more than ever now. Follow me to Rimrock!"

"Our going is slow Kanti, just so you know."

"Who are you?"

"My name is Ipsusnute, that is who I am."

"You are Ipsusnute?"

"Yes."

"You are the descendant of the ancient one?"

"Yes."

"That, my young human, is a very good sign. Come! No time to waste."

"Look, Grandpa, above the trees, there are hawks and eagles soaring."

Kanti, responding to Sofia's comments, landed on another branch.

"There are a couple of buzzards up there as well. We will need them too. What you cannot see are the coyotes and bobcats sliding through the underbrush below. With your help, I think we are ready. The only thing we lack is the element of surprise. We are waiting for them to arrive. I would like to position you in the grassy area in the middle of Rimrock. Many of the villagers will be directed to stay in their burrows with doors closed. Some able squirrels have sharp sticks and will defend the village from within if need be. All these predators I bring with me, above and below, I will be positioned outside of the walls."

It was late morning when Sofia, Nute, Walter, and Kanti, arrived at the walls of Rimrock. All of the village squirrels were scrambling around in preparation for the assault.

What Dennis and the rats did not understand was what they were actually headed for. The creatures of the canyon had united. This would not be just about rat versus squirrel and how to get rid of rodents, as Dennis had hoped.

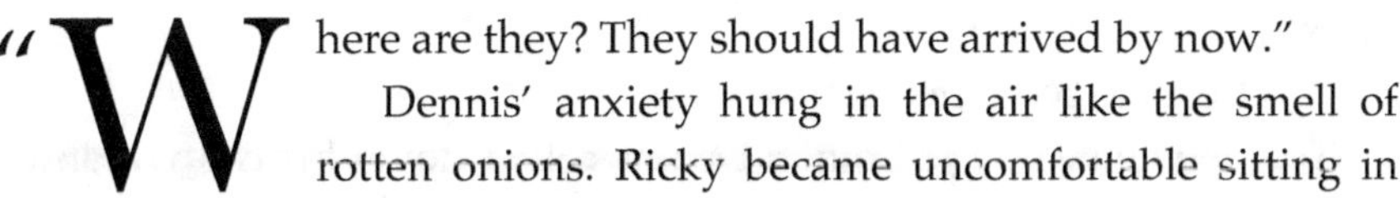

"Where are they? They should have arrived by now."

Dennis' anxiety hung in the air like the smell of rotten onions. Ricky became uncomfortable sitting in the cab with Dennis.

"I'd wait outside," he said. "May I?"

"I wouldn't stand out there. The rats can't be trusted. Go sit in the back of the truck and stay out of trouble."

An hour passed. There was no sign. And then Ricky began to hear movement. Farther off at first. Then, what sounded like the rustling of grass and brush, became a roar, as thousands of rats approached. Somehow, over the winter and early spring, they had multiplied.

They had spawned an entire fighting force. Sleg had not given any thought of where he might put them all, or how he would feed them. He just wanted them to fight. It didn't take long for the young rats to learn the way of their colony. Among the rats, it was only a choice between eating or be eaten. Each young rat believed that attacking and taking over was the only way to satisfy their hunger and hatred.

The rats swarmed and poured into the turn-around, completely surrounding Dennis' truck. The large mound of boulders that held the Pine Stone Inn was now an island in a sea of rats. The door was closed, locked, with the large wooden beam in place. Those inside huddled quietly, aware of the horror just outside their doors. There was more than one door to the Pine Stone Inn, the other one had double doors. It was where barrels and foodstuffs arrived, but it was now boarded up and barricaded as well. The beaver stood at that entrance, making sure it was secure.

Outside, Eek had made his way to the truck just under the window where Dennis peered out.

"Where have you been? We've been waiting!" Dennis shouted.

"There were some weasels, a badger, and a coyote. We had to go way around, down by the river. We lost some anyway. No matter. Plenty more," Eek reported.

Dennis' was exasperated. "I never said that this would be easy!"

The screeches and squeaks of thousands of rats were almost deafening. Sleg was sitting on one side of the island of boulders that held the Pine Stone Inn, above the sea of rats, unaware of the precious sanctuary within.

"SILENCE!" screeched Sleg.

The obedient mob fell quiet. Dennis rolled down his cab window, not about to step out. Ricky now stood amongst the large containers of rat poison that were Dennis' reward awaiting the rats for their defeat of the squirrels. He was shocked and horrified by the enormous mass of rats surrounding him.

"Now, where is this Rimrock?" Sleg's voice was filled with the sound of vengeful contempt.

"We wait for it to become darker. Rimrock is just around the bend," Dennis assured.

"Show us!" demanded Sleg.

"I will lead you there."

Dennis had no intention of doing anything of the kind. His plan was to get them all riled up to the point of becoming so berserk that even Sleg wouldn't be able to stop them.

"Did you bring the poison?" Dennis asked Ricky.

"I did. Are you really going to poison all these rats?"

"Of course, you idiot! You didn't think that, once they rid us of the squirrels, I would let them live, do you?"

19

CHANGE OF PLANS

Teek and the others awoke at the earliest sign of light. They were now on sacred ground. All the animals of the canyon had left the gathering while it was still dark. Low rumbling snorts and neighs caught the squirrels' attention. Heavy hoofed footfalls walked up to them.

"You are still here," one horse said.

"You have a keen ability to notice the obvious!" said the other.

"I don't know what else to say. How can we help them?"

"I have an idea!" It was Peeps.

"What, Peeps?" Teek asked.

Peeps walked up to the horses. "Hello, I am Peeps."

"I am Buster, and this here is Billy."

"Buster, will you let us climb onto your back? Can you carry us back to the road? It sure would go faster. Not that we would want you to go fast, mind you, I just mean that if you could carry us, we could get there sooner."

"Happy to. That is what we do! I will kneel down, Billy, what do you say? Can these two ride on your back?"

"Sure, I can take a couple."

"Brilliant, Peeps!" Teek commended.

"Alright then. Hop on," said Buster, "You ready? You might hold on to our manes, it would be a long way down for you. Try to stay in the middle of our back. Billy has quite a pronounced dorsal stripe, he does not like to talk about it."

"You be quiet, Buster!"

"See?"

Teek looked at the others. "Cicci, you are with me on Buster. Then, Peeps and Digger, you are on Billy."

The two horses knelt down on their forelegs in the manner of trained horses.

"Here. Climb up the nearside."

"Which side?" asked Digger.

"Oh, no matter. You can figure it out. Hang on!"

"Woo-hoo, my this is quite something!" Cicci exclaimed, grasping tightly to the mane, almost slipping off as the horses stood back up. "I can see why the humans like it so much. Buster, you are a moving mountain!"

"I have never thought much about my size. I can see how you would though, with the size you are and all."

The squirrels jostled back and forth on the horse's shoulders as they walked to the fence at the edge of the road. After a short while, the ride was over, and the horses stood at the fence, facing the road.

"You live down there somewhere in that canyon?"

"Yes, we do," answered Teek. "May we trouble you a while longer?"

"No trouble."

"Do you think you could stay here for just a bit longer and look out for any fast-moving beasts?"

"We will!" The horses looked at each other.

"What is he talking about? Trucks and cars?" Billy asked Buster.

"Anything that might run them over, I am guessing."

The horses knelt down, so that the squirrels could scamper off.

Once down, Teel looked back up at Buster, with relief, "Thank you! I just cannot tell you how much difference that made for us."

"We will stay here and watch out for... 'beasts.' When you hear me neigh, that means you are clear to go."

The squirrels darted swiftly across the road upon hearing Buster's neigh and didn't stop until they reached a large sage on the other side.

"Ow! Why you!"

Billy had wheeled around and bitten Buster on the butt and was now headed back to the barn in a dead run.

"Wait until I catch you, we will see how fast you can run after that!" Buster's voice trailed off as he ran after Billy.

"Well, all right then. That was interesting. Look at them go." Cicci said, watching them run back to the barn.

"Onward!" said Teek.

"Teek?"

"Yes, Cicci."

"I was just thinking, if that otter is there with that raft to help us across the river when we arrive, we may be able to make it back to the Pine Stone Inn before it gets dark. Then we can head toward Rimrock from there when the bright light of day appears over the cliff.

"Let us hope that works out," Cicci. "I like that idea."

They headed down into the canyon. The squirrels scrambled the entire way down until they reached the flat rock at the edge of the river. There they all drank their fill of the familiar flavor of river water, a long overdue thirst quencher.

There was the otter, waiting to meet them. She popped her head out of the water, crunching on a crayfish.

"I heard you were—" *Crunch, crunch.* "—headed back this way. Figured that this might be—" *Crunch, crunch, crunch.* "—a good place to be."

"Oh yes, thank you. I..." began Teek.

The otter had quickly slipped back into the water to retrieve the raft to carry them back across the deep pool.

"She sort of reminds me of Fisk," commented Peeps.

"Only more reliable," Cicci added.

"I like Fisk. He lives a great life, that one," Digger added.

He had been quiet for some time. Digger's perspective was always sort of independently his own. He seemed to frequently have something different to say.

"We all like Fisk, Digger," Teek corrected.

"Okay, hop on," the otter said as she pulled the raft up to the rock. The deep, dark water swirled around and over the large slab of bark, flooding over the squirrel's feet.

Cicci stared at the water she waded in. "I do not remember this raft sitting so low in the water."

Teek noticed that the raft looked like it may have gotten harder to pull. She may need a new one soon. "I am sure it will make it across this time."

Digger stared into the depths. He noticed shadowy shapes darting away from the raft. "What are those fast-moving shapes under us?"

"Fish, those are. Tasty, tasty, tasty!"

It was Fisk popping his head out of the water.

"Fisk! I... where did he go?" asked Cicci.

"Back under looks like," answered Peeps.

Soon Fisk re-surfaced. In his mouth was a sizable trout.

"Issis wa yo a eeing. Iss ool iss ull o ees."

The squirrels looked at each other, quite puzzled. Fisk dropped the fish.

"Sorry, I was trying to say, that 'this is what you were seeing, and that this pool is full of them.'"

"You dropped the fish,"

"Yup, yup, Peeps, I did, I did, could not speak with it. No matter, I have eaten my first meal. I can catch 'em pretty easy. I catch 'em fast."

"Fisk?"

"Yes, Teek."

"Do you have a moment? I would like to ask you a question."

"Well, speak up and ask!"

"Well, I would, but I could not find the right moment. Do you know the otter that is pulling this raft?"

"I should say I do! That is my older sister, Jabber, she does not speak much."

Peeps glanced at Teek, then over at Jabber, then back at Fisk, and was about to reply, when Teek held up a paw in anticipation of Peeps' next comment.

"Be sure to thank her if we do not get the chance. It is so important that we return to Rimrock in a hurry. Have you heard?"

"Oh yes, I have heard... I have. Rats, rats, rats everywhere! I am also on my way there. I will swim of course. I hear that Walter Prudy has returned to help."

"Walter is there?" Teek's eyes widened. He looked at Cicci, elated. "Then we need to hurry!"

"I still think it is best to hole up at the entrance to the passage that leads to the cavern of Ahtūn." Cicci reminded.

"All right, but we will have to start all that much earlier."

"I had best be going then, yup, I should go. Need to find the family upriver before heading to Rimrock, let them know 'n all."

"Alright Fisk, I..."

Fisk had submerged. Jabber was suddenly bumped from underneath the water. She let out a squeak and then a hiss. Fisk's head didn't resurface until he was up-river some distance. He looked back with a grin and dove back under. Jabber shook her head as she pulled them closer to a more familiar shore.

"Is that? It is! That crayfish that summonses Ahtūn! It is sitting on the opposite side of that rock, do you see? How did it know we would be returning?" asked Cicci.

"That is what he does, I guess," answered Teek.

"It is good to see that it escaped Jabber's appetite," added Peeps.

The raft pulled up to the stone dock at the entrance to the passageway back into the cavern of Ahtūn.

As they hopped onto the rock from the raft, Peeps commented, "Do not look down."

Of course, once his words were spoken, everyone looked down at the deep swirling water between the raft and the stone dock.

"Thank you for that, Peeps, very helpful, as usual." Cicci made an especially long hop to shore, for fear of falling short.

Peeps stared at the crustacean as they passed. It stood quite still, but for the flicking of its antennae. Then it crawled into the water.

"Heading to the cavern I imagine, to announce our return." Digger observed.

"Yes, Digger, I believe you are right."

The sounds of the thunderous water echoed off the smooth walls of lava as they made their way back through the cool, damp passage. The same musty, moist smells greeted them once again.

"Stay close. Let us not forget. This passage has danger."

"Hey, watch it! You nearly stepped on me! I oughta knock you over!"

"What is going on up there!" Teek called ahead.

"It is not us! I do not know who said that," replied Digger.

"Down here! What is the matter with you? I am right here! I will move over here so you can see. That way, we can face-off properly!"

There was a shaft of light that shone down through a crack in the ceiling of the passage, from the bright light above. Into that spot of light, the spider hopped, reared up on its four back legs and stared up at Digger with its eight shiny, and tiny black eyes.

"All right smart guy, take your best shot!"

It was a quick and rather tiny jumping spider. No bigger than a pinky fingernail.

"Excuse me? You are just a..." started Digger.

"Just a what? Come on, let us do this! Or are you afraid?"

"I am not, um... hey, Teek?!"

Teek scooted by Cicci and Peeps and joined Digger at his side.

"What is happening here?"

"I will tell you what is happening here. He almost stepped on me!"

"We are not here to fight. We are just passing through. May we continue?"

The spider paused, then said, "I tell you what. You tell your clumsy friend here to watch where he is going!"

"Hey, I am not..."

"We shall be more careful, sir. I am Teek, what is your name?"

"Tap!"

"Tap? Alright, Tap. We shall be careful. If you will now excuse us, we are in a bit of a hurry."

"Yes, well, no doubt the reason for the clumsiness!"

"No doubt. Come along Digger, keep moving." Teek lifted his gaze and looked down his nose at Digger with a little smile.

"Not much further, everyone, let us start to prepare ourselves for the cavern and that narrow ledge. We do not know if it is submerged or above water."

Soon, Teek peered into the cavern from the opening of the passageway. The cavern and the pool were illuminated once again by the light beaming down from the opening where the water spilled into the pool. There, back on the ledge on the opposite side of the pool, the crayfish was back at its post, waiting for them. Teek turned.

"It is back."

"It is fast!" replied Peeps. "It is rather large, is it not? It must be too big to eat."

"By an otter?" Digger reminded him.

"Maybe the ancient human keeps him alive, like he does Ahtūn."

"I am thinking that maybe it needs to announce us to Ahtūn. Otherwise, Ahtūn might forget who we are and eat us."

The crayfish turned and tapped on the stone wall behind it.

"Bing, bing, bing" then again, *"bing, bing, bing."*

Ahtūn surfaced immediately, as though he were already near the surface.

"Bing, bing..."

The crayfish stopped his tapping abruptly as Ahtūn spun around in a suddenly aggressive and threatening manner.

"I see them! Stop binging! Next time he has a softshell, I will..." He gurgled as the water spilled and sputtered from his jaws.

"Ahtūn, it is I, Teek, and the others. We need to return to Rimrock. The rats are advancing on our village."

The giant fish gurgled again. "Yes, Teek, the rats are almost there."

"What did he say? How does he know this?" Peeps asked.

"Peeps! Just listen. Be quiet!"

Ahtūn continued in his quiet, gurgling voice "The rats travel by way of the river. There are many. Some of them stopped to drink. I smell them and taste them in the water. I know where they are. You may pass. I will not harm you. The water is low... below the ledge. You may go to the other passage."

"So, we have all that going for us," added Peeps.

Teek quickly turned and glared at Peeps, who looked down and lifted both paws in surrender.

"We will just keep moving then. Thank you for letting us pass."

"Now that you know this place, you must return, and bring something for me, like a worm, a beetle maybe, more flies, or maybe a grasshopper, whatever you can find."

"You can depend upon us, Ahtūnowhiho."

"Yes, I can." Then, he submerged.

They traveled single file once again, past the sucking whirlpool, and past the deep swirling river water flowing through the cavern. They could see Ahtūn in the water below them slipping alongside them, following them.

"If there was ever a reminder not to fall in, it would be right now. He makes me nervous," said Peeps.

"Very true, Peeps," Cicci confirmed.

"Just make sure you watch your step and not find out what he would do if you fell in. When he told us before that he would eat anyone who met that fate, I believed him. The narrow path is still wet and slippery, so be extra careful. It is when you stop thinking about danger that something happens."

They made it to the opening of the passage with great relief and ducked in quickly. There, they huddled together to recover.

"Will, um, will we be passing this way again, Teek?"

"I do not know, Cicci. I cannot think of a reason why we would, but then, it is hard to predict. Can you all stay here? I shall return in a minute."

"Where are you going?"

"Back. Your question reminded me that I need to find out more before leaving this place."

Teek returned to the opening of the passage to the cavern. Ahtūn was just under the surface waiting for him. He lifted his head from the water.

"There is more for you to know," he gurgled. "I smelled something very bad in the water. It made me dive deep. It was poison. Someone must have rinsed a cup of it out in the river. I do not know its purpose, but I do know that it comes from a human."

"It can only be that human, Dennis Digwood. I shall give this much thought and tell the others."

"One more thing," added Ahtūn. "There is another chamber, only this one is not filled with water. There is an opening to another passage halfway up this one that leads to it. From there it continues to the burial chamber of the ancient spirit human. But this chamber is not that one. This chamber is deep... very deep. So deep that it holds a very hot liquid. You must come back. There is something in that cavern that you must take to the burial chamber. Go now to save your village, the rats are close. This was told to me. Now I tell you."

Teek returned to Cicci and the others.

"Teek, did you find out more?"

"Yes, we have less time than we thought. We may rest for a little while, but then we must press on to Rimrock. We should head to the top of this passage now. I will explain then."

They climbed back up the passage. Teek stopped halfway up at the opening of the branching-off passage and peered in. There was nothing that could be seen in the dark blackness of the opening. There *was* noticeably warmer air flowing from it, along with a curious smell. He was not sure that he had smelled this the first time. Smells have vivid memories attached to them. He could recall something about an egg, broken on a rock, rotting in the sun, something Kanti had mentioned to Ahtūn. Ever so quietly and through the distant depths of the passage-way, he could hear that old familiar rhythmic beat. It was barely there. Still, it signaled him, not to enter, but somehow, not with words, telling him to move on. He stood for a moment while the rest stared at him.

"Alright, let us go."

"Something tells me that this other passageway is in my future!" Peeps looked back at the opening to the passage as he headed up toward the bright opening at the top of the main passage.

"We may stop here for a short while and nibble on whatever is left in our satchels. From this point on, I must tell you, things will be dangerous. I have complete faith in all of you that you are brave, careful, and thoughtful squirrels. But we must be extra careful now. Everything will be alright if we stick together. Cicci, please stay next to me. Nap now if you can. It will be some time before you will be able to again. Nobody is safe from this point on. Not even in the village of Rimrock. Fortunately, we have many other defenders of our canyon on our side. Let them handle this, you all just stay clear of trouble. There is much more for all of us to do after this is over. Ahtūn has told me that we must come back and find something important in another cavern."

"I knew it!"

"Peeps, I am much more concerned about where we are headed for right now. If you find yourself headed down another dark tunnel soon, you are very fortunate. Now, all of you rest while you can."

"I do not rest! I wait!"

"We all need rest!" replied Teek.

"Teek, none of us said that."

"But I clearly heard..."

"Wait. Tap? Is that you?"

"Of course, it is me! Do you think I would miss this?"

"But what are we going to do with..."

"Do not mind me. I shall hang on to a satchel. You will not even notice me."

"That was the point, was it not?" said Digger.

"Do not start with me, squirrel. I will finish it!"

Digger dropped his head then turned to peer out at the opening.

Teek continued. "Well, you are here now. One never knows from where greatness comes."

The group settled down to take a rest and to think about the ominous way ahead. Not one of them slept, except Digger, for a while. Tap hopped off the satchel he had been clinging to and sat on a rock looking out ahead. Teek joined him. Tap reared up and looked at him.

"So, what are we headed for?"

"I do fear the horrible thing that we may be headed for, Tap. I fear for all involved. Except for maybe the bigger predators. It should be a pretty good day for them. The days of Rimrock being hidden and protected are over. You are a brave one. Your heart is larger than your size. I do not look forward to this destination."

"Maybe that is because you know more about what will happen."

"Yes, well, the more you know, the more things you have to worry about, I suppose. We should rest no more. I cannot just stay here."

"I cannot either, Teek." It was Cicci joining them at the opening. "This is not what I would call rest. I would rather be moving toward Rimrock."

"Go rouse the other two. Tap, hop on. What you will soon see should shake even you."

Cicci found Peeps and Digger sitting up against the wall of the passage, staring at the opposite wall.

"Are you ready?"

"As we shall ever be," answered Peeps. "Digger was sharing some insights as to what may be ahead. My thoughts are darker than ever now."

"Peeps," Cicci put her paw on his shoulder. "Things are rarely as bad as our thinking makes them. We will watch out for each other. And do not forget all the animals are there to help us. I have been giving this some thought, and I have determined, now mind you I have not had a chance to speak to Teek about it, but it seems to me that the first thing you should do when you arrive back in the village, Peeps, is to find your momma Meep. Then you, your momma, and Digger, should all go to hide in Stonewood Place. You may know of another place you'd rather be, but if not, go there. We have found a tunnel."

As the group scrambled up the slope and upriver, Cicci spoke softly into Teek's ear. She reminded him of the tunnel that he and Digger had located before their journey, adding that it might be a good hiding place, if need be, for the two of them, for Peeps, Meep, and Digger, or anyone else for that matter.

"Yes, good thinking, Cicci. It may not come to that, but you are right."

The squirrels found a small deer trail leading upriver and followed it. Digger scampered up to Teek, grasping his front leg. "Look down at the ground, Teek. Tracks, thousands of them. There are so many, and they are fresh, and I can still smell them. They just passed this way."

"Alright, listen to me each of you. No talking and watch your step, no noise. The rats are just ahead."

They followed the deer trial by the river in silence.

"Teek!" Digger whispered. "Over here." Teek and Cicci found Digger and Peeps over by a grey squirrel that lay dead. It had been scratched and bitten by many assailants.

"Poor fella. There will be much more of this before the night is through."

"I have seen this sort of thing before..." it was Tap speaking up. "Mostly floating down the river. Sometimes I hop out onto that dock rock. You would be surprised to see what floats by occasionally."

Just what we need... a bolder Peeps, Teek thought to himself.

"How many dead spiders have you seen?" asked Digger.

"That is it. Let me at him!"

"Hey, hold on, I am just saying that it is a bit different when it is your own kind!"

"I did not like the tenor of that comment!"

"Keep moving," ordered Teek. "Clearly, we are getting close."

As they rounded a corner along the bank of the river, the small deer trail cut through a grassy spot. Off to the upriver side, was a group of large rats all circled around something. They were all chattering at once and so didn't notice the approaching squirrels. Teek immediately made a ditch sign in silence. Peering out from under some boulders, they watched and listened. It was Sleg, Eek, and several attendant rats bringing up the rear of the mass of marauding rats. They had surrounded a small mouse and were about to kill it and eat it.

"Please, no! I told you, I do not know where Rimrock is. I do not travel up that way!"

"Up what way?"

No, do not say it, Pip! Teek shut his eyes as this thought raced through his mind. He knew the little mouse. It was Pip the mouse whom he had met at the Pine Stone Inn. The one that had bravely sworn allegiance to him.

"He lies... kill him!"

"No, please, I have little ones!"

Brave little guy, Teek thought.

Sleg's screeching scratchy voice could then be heard. "Well, perhaps we will find them too, they would make a nice snack!"

Pip was horrified. He crouched, shivering uncontrollably. Quite suddenly, appearing from the nearby trees, a large black bird swooped repeatedly down with loud croaking sounds. The rats scattered in different directions, and the little mouse managed to scurry under a rock. It was Kanti.

"Kanti! Are we ever glad to see you! Is Walter here?"

"Walter is at Rimrock with Sofia and Ipsusnute."

"Ipsusnute? Who is that?"

"I will explain when you get there. Now you must hurry!"

"You saved Pip! Thank you, Kanti," said a grateful Cicci.

"I only wish I had been able to finish the job. Soon I will! You must not stay here. Keep moving to the protection of Rimrock. We guard the walls. Oh, and do not step in it."

"Step in what?" asked Peeps.

After a long stare at Peeps, Kanti answered his question.

"Never mind."

"Pip? Are you in there?"

"I am here."

"Come out, it is safe now. Well, it is safer anyway. Come with us to Rimrock."

"I must return to my burrow and my family but thank you. I have spread the word as best I can to smaller animals and some birds. The more that know, the better, right?"

"Yes Pip, you are right. I am so glad that Kanti showed up when he did and that you are still with us."

"I am glad as well, for my family. We live near here. I should be alright now. I will stay undercover. It was just a misfortune that they found me."

Kanti replied, "Well, they are about to find some misfortune of their own. Follow me now, little ones, I will make sure that your way is clear to Rimrock."

"If Sleg and those other rats are headed toward Rimrock, that is not good, is it?" asked Teek.

Kanti clarified by adding, "Actually, I think it is. It is better to have them closer together than to have them all spread out. Now, follow me."

"What is this? Oh, ick! I stepped in it!" declared Peeps.

"Stepped in what Peeps?" asked Cicci.

"I think it is rat dung! It is everywhere!"

"Let us go, everyone. Watch your step!" Teek directed.

Teek, Cicci, Peeps, Digger, and Tap rounded the corner, and there was Dennis Digwood, waiting for them with a large killing stick in his hands. The clearing was a large one with no place to ditch from certain death.

"Well, well, well. Surprise! Don't bother playing dumb. Oh yes, I can understand you, remember? You need to hold your little voices down; someone might hear you. So, one of you would be that Teek squirrel. Finally, we meet. Well, you are all the little troublemakers. It seems clear to me that if I take care of you, your other little friends will have no one to lead them. Then the rats can have the rest. Ah, ah, ah. Don't try to ditch, you'll be dead before you take a step. If you think I'm going to let some little squirrels keep me from the project of my life, think again, before I blow you all to bits. Hold still, I don't want to maim you, I want to kill you."

"You don't want to kill us, Dennis," said Teek.

"I don't? I may understand what you say when you speak, but that doesn't mean you are my equals. I am superior to you, you're just a bunch of little rodents! Do you think this part of the country is available for just anyone to live in? I will be famous someday. This will be a park or a golf course. There will be a statue of me. You are nothing and will continue to be nothing."

"Rodents, right?" asked Peeps.

"Yes, just rodents. Everyone around here respects me. They don't even know, or care, that you squirrels exist!"

"That all depends on whom you ask," replied Teek.

"This canyon is mine to develop and sell. I just need to get rid of you. Time's up."

He raised his shotgun. A screech rang out. Sharp talons dug into Dennis' back. He screamed and reeled around in pain. Kanti had alerted Apitah, the young Muha (red-tailed hawk), to the danger, having watched it develop from above. Apitah swooped down just in time to sink his razor-like talons into Dennis' back, saving the lives of the four squirrels. The gun went off, into the air, harmlessly missing everyone. The squirrels ditched in all directions, finding cover out of sight. Teek and Cicci found cover under a boulder covered by heavy brush. They stayed motionless and silent as Dennis continued to scream, crawling up the hill to his truck and ultimately, the local hospital.

"Wow, we really owe that bird a lot. First, he saves us from Ish the gopher snake, and now this," Teek reflected.

"Something tells me that he might have been alerted by someone we know very well," Cicci replied. "Is he gone yet?"

"Kkkkk not yet," came a familiar croaking voice.

"I knew this was you're doing!" Cicci acknowledged and thanked Kanti for being there for them again and saving their lives.

"Well, you little ones tend to get in a lot of trouble, so I need to keep a close eye on you. Besides, we have a lot to do. Let us wait here for another moment until Dennis Digwood drives away. Where's Peeps and Digger?"

"Over here," Digger replied.

Peeps was visibly shaking. Digger, although unnerved and quite focused and serious, was doing better. They darted, starting, and stopping in frightened and nervous movements of squirrels as they came over to where Teek, Cicci, and Kanti were at the edge of the clearing.

"It should be alright to continue now."

They all looked up into a tree to find Apitah sitting proudly, looking down at another successful attack. Kanti let out a loud croak of thanks, as Apitah lifted off and back up into the clouds. Kanti took special notice of Peeps condition.

"I have been thinking. Peeps, what would you say about a flight back to Rimrock?"

Peeps looked up with surprise and delight. "You mean, on your back?"

"You'd have to hold on tight. I think we should get you back right now. The rest can walk. How about it?"

"Well, I, I, that would be most fine indeed!" said Peeps as he stood and stared in wonder at Kanti.

"Hop on then. Like I said, hold on tight. Oh, and you probably should not mention this to your momma. I will drop you off at the entrance to Rimrock and you can scramble in the rest of the way."

Cicci glanced at Teek and then smiled warmly at Kanti. She knew that Kanti was offering this special gift to Peeps out of kindness and caring. After all the jabs, it was a very kind offer, so Peeps climbed carefully onto the back of the large black bird.

"Now grab my feathers just behind my neck and hold on. The take-off will be, well, rather rough and sudden, maybe even a bit shocking. You are no doubt the only squirrel who has ever flown. At least on the back of a bird."

If a squirrel could have grinned from ear to ear, Peeps would have.

"Here we go..."

Peep's beaming face momentarily changed to a look of shock with the first beats of Kanti's powerful wings. They lifted off and Peeps looked down on his friends beaming once again.

"See you back in Rimrock," he squeaked. He had never been more thrilled.

Teek, Cicci, Digger, and Tap headed upriver until they arrived at a most familiar bend. It was all very strangely quiet as they approached the outer walls. Kanti landed on a branch just above them.

"Little ones do not let the silence fool you. Everyone is in position. Remember many of them are well trained in predation. Silence is their tactic, power, speed, and sharp teeth and claws are their weapons. We are ready. There are many eyes on you right now so you may go into the village without worry. There you will find everyone waiting for you."

THE BATTLE FOR RIMROCK

There was never a stranger, nor a more welcome sight, than to see Walter, Sofia, and Ipsusnute all sitting together on the central grassy area. But Teek only noticed Walter at first. He scrambled over and leaped onto Walter's lap.

"Now I know everything will be alright. I might as well be sitting on the lap of Ipsusnute himself!"

"You almost are."

"How so?"

"Teek, I would like you to meet Ipsusnute. This young man is the descendant of Ipsusnute, the ancient human spirit that lived long ago and now looks over this canyon. This young one's name is also Ipsusnute."

Teek had no words. He could not help but approach the young human male and stare into his face, and into his eyes.

"I must show you your ancestor's burial chamber," said Teek. "It is under a field of boulders. There must have been an entrance for you long ago, but now it has been covered. I thought I just happened to find it, but now I believe I was directed by the ancient one, your ancestor. I now stand before a powerful line of humans. Surely the bright light of day is shining upon us. Ipsusnute!"

"You can call me Nute, Teek."

Teek turned to Walter. "You are actually here. I did not know if I would ever see you again, Walter! We owe everything to you! Cicci and I owe our very lives to you and Sofia! It is so good to see you both again. Thank you for your help and friendship!"

"My honor, Teek. This is the most important moment in my life, my dear friend. This is the most important thing I can do."

"I see you brought some pretty solid tapping sticks."

"Today they may be used as war clubs. This is nothing I ever wanted my granddaughter to be a part of." Walter turned to Sofia. "Don't breathe a word of this to your mother."

"You know me better than that, Grandpa."

Nute addressed Walter quietly. "We must all have a little warrior in us today!"

"I agree!" came a voice from no one they could see.

"Who was that?" asked Walter.

"That," said Teek, "is Tap."

"Tap?"

"Yes," answered Teek. "Typically, you will hear him before you see him."

"What do you mean? I am right here!"

Teek tipped his head, and turned his eyes, in the direction of a small boulder next to Walter. Walter looked at the boulder.

"Down here!"

Walter looked down to see the tiny Tap reared up on four back legs, looking up at him with eight shiny black eyes.

"Do not look so surprised. Have you never seen something like me before?"

Walter turned to Sofia. He didn't quite know what to say, and so he said the obvious. "That's a jumping spider."

"It appears so, Grandpa. Good thing we know he's there."

"He hopped onto one of our satchels and came along for the, the, well, the 'battle' I guess."

"Okay, welcome Tap, all the best tonight!"

"Indeed!"

"Grandpa, I brought a blanket along. Let me lay it over your shoulders. I don't want you getting chilled."

Seek appeared from the double doors of Colony Hall. He headed directly to the central grassy area as Kanti was just landing. He somehow knew right when Kanti was going to appear.

The light was starting to dim. Some clouds had rolled in, but they parted to reveal a large, full moon that illuminated everything like a spotlight. It was so bright, that everything cast a moon shadow.

Although there was still light in the sky from the remains of the day, it was clear that if the clouds cleared, everything could be lit and clearly visible.

"Kanti, tell us of any news."

"I have much to report. Flying overhead, some eagles and hawks have just told me that the rats are getting closer as they search for Rimrock. Fortunately, it does not appear they know exactly where to go. But I must warn you, there are many of them, far more than I imagined there would be. All of us must prepare ourselves for the attack. I know that you want to defend your own village, but I suggest that you find a place to hide and let us handle this. You are all so brave, and yet you are also so precious to us, you must be protected, and we are better able to do this than you. Hopefully, we can keep them out of Rimrock. Walter, Sofia, Ipsusnute, you are here to defend the village from any rats that might get through. There should be no need for any of these four squirrels to fight, so you four must now go to your burrows and stay hidden."

"But Kanti, I..." Teek started, but Kanti cut him off.

"Do as I say!"

"Yes, Kanti."

"Go to your burrow and stay there. Do not come out until this is over. Do you all understand? As difficult as this may be for you, your safety is the most important thing to this colony. If I knew before what I know now, I am not sure I would have wanted you to go on your journey. But now that you have gotten this far, and have done all you have done, we will see this through. It is what the ancient human spirit wants. I go now to check in on those brave and capable animals that surround your walls."

With that, he lifted into the air with three beats of his wings and disappeared over the edge of the cliffs.

"Well, I suppose that the best place for us is in the tunnel behind the wall in our beloved Stonewood Place. Walter, you have been my guardian. Again, you come to save me. I thank you. And now we must go underground."

"I would be nowhere else. The honor is all mine. You go. We will be here for you. Everything will be fine."

⋘◆⋙

Kanti landed on a branch above the hidden defenders of Rimrock. He addressed one of the coyotes who had shown up with her pack. She was the matriarch and the alpha female of the pack. Tonight, they had come to attack rats. She was also leading many of the other predators into the fight.

"Have you seen anything yet?" Kanti asked.

"Nothing, Kanti."

Kanti called to all the animals surrounding Rimrock. "Are you all listening? I have something to say."

A roar lifted above the boulders and brush, from every animal, and from under the branches, and the sky from every bird of prey.

"Hear me!" said Kanti, "This is the most important thing I have ever said! Many may fall at your side, but they shall not overcome us. Your eyes only have to behold to see the reward of the wicked! You all know what to do. You do what you do best."

All was silent. They waited and waited. There was nothing. There was only the sound of the wind and the river. They looked out over the hill but there was nothing.

"Where do you suppose they are?" one marmot asked a raccoon.

Kanti looked up at the hawks and eagles soaring overhead. No sign was signaled. Then there was a sudden screech from Apitah high above. He had spotted them. The rats were advancing.

Apitah tucked his wings and dove in the direction of their location, signaling Kanti.

Still the defenders waited and waited. Everything was strangely quiet. No sound of birds, only the wind and the distant roar of rapids... or was it something else? The sound could be part of the roar of the rapids.

At first it was way off and quiet, but it increased as the mass of marauding rats came closer. Increasingly louder and louder, they heard screeching, clawing, and scratching.

Then, the sound became a loud roar. The advancing rats poured over the hill, like a floodgate opening.

How could there be so many? Thousands and thousands of rats.

A wave of scrambling rats of all shapes and sizes swept down the slope, so many that the defenders needed to stop and watch in amazement before reacting. A thundering roar was advancing and advancing quickly, like a giant waterfall.

"Now!" Kanti croaked loudly.

There was no reaction from the defenders as they all watched in amazement.

"Now!" he called out again.

As if the canyon animals had awoken from a trance, they came alive.

Kanti loudly croaked his orders, "We must all attack at once, it is our only hope! We must slow them down."

The first wave of rats was met with coyotes, bobcats, otters, and badgers, along with smaller predators like minks, fishers, and martins. The fighting was savage, and the rats had the advantage, overwhelming the defenders with sheer numbers, there were three or four rats on every defender.

But then the raptors, other birds of prey, and buzzards began their attack. Even jays, magpies, and nutcrackers joined in the attack. Wave upon wave of hawks, eagles, buzzards, osprey, and all kinds of lesser birds of prey descended on the mass of rats.

Screams rose from the ranks of the rats as scores of them were plucked from above by sharp and deadly talons. Each time the claws closed on a rat's back like sharp-pointed knives, they were killed and dropped into the river. Some were taken high in the air and dropped on jagged rocks.

"Do you hear, Teek? The sound of the battle!" announced Tap.

"I do, but I am glad we are in here, and not out there!"

"I am not! I want to be out there!" It was Tap's declaration of war.

"Tap! I cannot imagine you, oh, never mind." Teek began.

"What? I'll show you!"

"Tap? No, do not!"

He was gone.

The squirrels looked at each other. They didn't know what to make of the actions of their new little friend.

Peeps felt that the silence should be broken, and so he began, "Well, he sure is an excitable little fellow, is he not?"

Outside of the walls of Rimrock, dead rats were everywhere. Not that there wasn't a few lurking inside the walls, but outside was simply nothing short of shocking. Yes, there were a few brave defenders that had been overwhelmed as well, but the rats had not anticipated that they would face such a united canyon of deadly animals.

The fight lasted through the night. The rats were fighting like they had nothing to lose, and they didn't. They had nothing to return to. It was Rimrock or nothing, except the wrath of Sleg. So, they fought on, tooth and claw.

Each type of animal fought its own type of fight, and this was an advantage because the rats all fought in the same manner.

One very brave and quite unexpected way to fight was a clever kind of deception. Two dozen rats traversed the edge of a cliff in the attack. Off to the edge of the cliff, they heard a voice calling out to them and challenging them to a fight.

"Hey, you! Mangy, greasy scum! Come over here and fight! I'll rip you to shreds!"

The two dozen rats charged toward the voice, but there was no animal that they could see, and it was too late. Their momentum took them right off the cliff to their deaths! All in all, that little voice would cause over a hundred rats to fall to their deaths that night. Quite an accomplishment for a tiny spider no bigger than a pinky fingernail. A little spider with a big heart.

Some rats made it through and were able to climb down into the center of the village. They came from the dark corners of the village, going from burrow to burrow. Most doors were barricaded, some burrows were empty. Village squirrels had found refuge in the inner refuges of the burrows and the hidden tunnels. Walter, Sofia, and Nute could see the glowing eyes of the rats sneaking into the village from dark corners. While the rats searched frantically for squirrels, they were set upon by guard squirrels with sharp sticks and three very aggressive and deadly humans with large sticks. Not one rat that made it over the wall of Rimrock survived the night. The tapping sticks had become war clubs and they found their mark time and time again until there were no more left alive.

Ten guard squirrels stood at the entrance of the village, facing out toward the narrow passage. From the outer opening at the other end of the passageway, they could hear the rats pour in. The screeching, clawing, and scratching sounds got closer and closer. The guard squirrels became frightened to the point of scampering away from the oncoming charge. But then there came a deep and thunderous roar. So loud and powerful was this roar that it caused the guard squirrels to fall over and scamper around in an attempt to ditch. There was more roaring and screeching, now mixed with screaming, many thudding, slapping, and scraping sounds. Then there was silence. The guard squirrels peered out from where they had ditched.

"Should we go see?" they asked each other. "Be careful. We do not know what we will find."

They advanced slowly, in the short, quick, starting and stopping way that ground squirrels make when they are cautious and unsure. Then they came around a bend in the passage and peered around the corner. There in the silvery moonlight lay hundreds of dead rats. Some still draped over a rock on the wall, many lay on the floor of the passage.

"What do you imagine happened?" one of the guard squirrels asked. "Something in the walls of this passage that we never speak of.

A powerful force that has guarded our passageway these many years. We had best return while we can!" said another.

The main battle was still going on outside of the walls of Rimrock. The dead and dying rats did not dissuade those still attacking. They scrambled over the top of their dead and kept coming. More canyon predators began to show up, hearing the sounds of battle. Badgers, minks, martins, and even Canada geese joined the fight. Canada geese, by the way, are fierce and formidable fighters. Bears showed up now that it was the middle of the night. Their powerful paws swatted four-to-five rats in one swipe. Bobcats and cougars set out on chases that the rats could not win, running down and pouncing on their foe in the way of wild cats.

"This is not right! What has happened? What are all of these things?" Screamed Sleg.

This outcome was not part of Sleg's plans. With that, he turned and waddled off hurriedly. Eek glanced at the attendant rats and scampered after him.

Dennis and Ricky stood on a nearby hill. This was an outcome they had not imagined. Only one thought hit Dennis between the eyes. His plans were being ruined before his eyes, along with the dwindling of his power and money. There was nothing left he could do. He raised his rifle and aimed at one of the bears. Before he was able to get a shot off, Nute was on him, ripping his gun away and knocking him down. Nute spun around to see Ricky sprinting back to the pickup truck, leaving his loyalty, and most likely his job, behind him. Ricky, the pickup, with the rat poison, sped away. Ricky wanted to find a local nightspot to sit and try to understand what had just happened.

Nute then stood over a dazed Dennis Digwood saying "You will never escape us, Dennis Digwood. You will not succeed. We will find you and defend our canyon and its creatures from you. You cannot hide as long as you intend to take over our canyon. You will not be able to resort to your laws. For whom will you call? The police? Animals? To whom will you say that you have sent rats to kill other animals in this canyon? What will you do with all that poison? Is that not more evidence of your wrongdoing? Is that not a crime against nature? No, we think you will go away and do your evil somewhere else!"

Nute ran back to rejoin the battle without waiting for a reply.

The hidden passageway behind a wall at Stonewood Place was surprisingly filled with villagers. Not just Digger's clan, and Peep's momma, Meep; but Cheeks and his momma, Teese, and his pappa Pinion. Seek made his way through many other villagers that had found out about the hidden tunnels, until he joined Teek and his group.

"It has become quite still out there. Do you think we should find out what has happened?" he asked Teek.

Teek turned and cracked open a couple of boards in the wall and peered through, down his hallway. The cool full light of night reflected off the shards of glass, casting shafts of blue light down his hall. All seemed quiet. At the other end of the hall, he could see his front door. It was open.

Curious, I thought I had closed it and secured it. Maybe in my haste, I had forgotten, or someone after me opened it again.

"Teek?" he heard behind him. It was Seek.

"It all seems to be over. I will go call to Walter," Teek whispered.

Teek slipped through the boards in the wall into his main hallway. The boards creaked under his paws as he crept carefully and slowly towards his front door. He could hear quiet whispers outside but could not determine their origin. The air around him was strangely still. He passed his largest room, near the front of the burrow. A living area that had seen many happy gatherings, now dark and silent. Then, he caught the sudden sound of scampering and claws scratching toward him. Startled, he spun around toward the sound, he could see two glowing eyes moving quickly toward him. He had little time to react before it was on him. His heart pounded with surprise and fright as the large rat ran over him, screeching and hissing. Teek was knocked back against the opposite wall of his hallway. The rat did not continue the attack, but rather headed for the door, and out it went.

Thump! Whack! Whack! Then silence again. Digger was first to scamper up to find Teek, behind him Cicci and Peeps, finally Digger.

"What happened? Are you all right?" Cicci was scrambling around so quickly that Teek could not actually tell what was going on enough to tell her.

"I... I do not know. A rat, I think? It was hiding in this front room and fled through the front door, and there, met its fate by our humans."

"Are you hurt?"

"No, I do not think so, it all happened so fast. I think it just wanted to escape. It ran right over me."

Cicci and Digger picked Teek up off the floor. Then they all turned their attention to the open front door. The light of night was still illuminating the village in a silvery cast and shone into Teeks front door. The first hint of the coming bright light was just starting to lighten the sky, but tiny points of light still filled it from one side of the Rimrock sky to the other. Three giant figures still sat, darkly silhouetted in the central grassy area. Laying just in front of his burrow, was the large rat. It had been slain as it fled. It hadn't gotten far.

"Walter Prudy?" Teek called out in the loudest whisper he could muster. "Walter Prudy?" he called again.

"Teek? Teek, is that you?"

"It is us. May we come out now?"

Silence was the answer.

Fwoop, fwoop, fwoop, fwoop. It was Kanti landing in the grass next to the humans. "It is all but finished. I say 'all but finished' because there are still a couple of unfinished, and rather unpleasant tasks for me. I must go take care of them now."

"Teek was calling to me. Should I tell him that it is alright for them to come out now?"

"It is alright for them to leave their burrows, but too soon for them to leave the protective walls of Rimrock."

"Teek!" Walter called. "It is alright for you to come out now but stay close to us."

With a *whoop, whoop, whoop,* Kanti was gone.

Teek, Cicci, Peeps, and Digger, made their way to the central grassy area in front of Walter, Sofia, and Nute. Seek soon appeared after them. The rest of the village would stay hidden until the bright light of day brought the reassurance of the ending of the night of terror. A night

that would be retold during Story Elder gatherings in Colony Hall, for
years to come.

"Where did Kanti fly off to?" asked Teek.

Walter answered, "There is a lot left to do. He went to... he's on his
way to..." began Walter.

Peeps spoke up in a faraway voice, still thinking back to his flying
experience. "You know, wherever he is going, he is probably there
already!"

Nute turned to the group of ground squirrels and spoke softly.

"Give us a minute if you would."

The squirrels turned to notice that Sofia was now in Walter's arms
with her head hanging low.

"What is wrong?" Teek asked. "Is Sofia hurt?"

Walter looked up toward Teek, shut his eyes, and shook his head to
indicate that they needed a moment. Nute moved over next to the
squirrels to explain.

"She was trying to help you and felt that your life was in danger.
Sofia was the one that killed the rat that was hiding in your burrow.
When it scrambled out the front door, she hit it several times with her
stick. Times such as these call on all of us to act quickly or suffer bad
things because of hesitation. My people have a history of being faced
with this sort of thing. Our homes were being invaded. Dark times
indeed, for everyone. It is against Sofia's nature to kill. It is against her
spirit. She is not a warrior."

"She may not be a warrior, but she is brave," replied Cicci.

Teek looked away, back toward the burrows. He noticed the faces of
the villagers peering through their doorways, wondering if it was safe.
It seemed to them as though nothing would be safe again, at least not
as they had understood it.

Teek turned back to Nute. "We will go attend to the villagers, then
we will come back."

From where Kanti floated, he could see the scene below from the night before. Animals of all varieties, on the ground and in the air, were busy carrying off the dead rats. Once, the many varieties of carrion-eating birds, coyotes, and other canyon critters could clear the area, all of this would be just an unpleasant memory.

Yet none of them could have hoped for a more decisive victory. There was actually more than saving Rimrock to celebrate. A community of canyon animals, both predator, and prey, had united and cooperated with each other to save a community. This would prove to be a powerful lesson, a new way to protect something that each of them held vital and precious, the canyon. The animals that called the canyon their home now understood that their unity and cooperation would have to be played out again on a much larger scale.

Kanti looked up from where he soared. Way above him flew another. It was Apitah the young red-tailed hawk. Kanti flew up to him.

"Kanti, you have led us well. I saw a group of rats head back toward the Pine Stone Inn. Shall we head in that direction?" asked Apitah.

"Let us do just that."

They turned and flew in the direction of the inn.

"Apitah, have you spotted Dennis Digwood, the human behind all of this?"

"We just flew over where I saw him fall at the hands of Ipsusnute, keeping him from killing a brave bear. But he was no longer there. He had gotten up and wandered off. He appeared to be confused... or maybe he was stunned."

"That one must be watched closely."

"Look! Down there!"

Sleg, Eek, and three attendant rats arrived at the boulder pile that held the Pine Stone Inn.

Apitah looked over at Kanti with a gleam in his eye. He was born a warrior. He was looking for one word from Kanti, and he would dive upon them.

That word came from Kanti, "I am not going to let that nasty 'ol rat ruin my favorite watering hole!"

That was all Apitah needed to hear.

"Apitah, wait, I should go..."

Apitah was much faster than a raven. In a blink, he was already a hundred feet below Kanti and heading directly toward the rats. As Apitah descended he noticed something fly by just underneath him. It was a female cooper's hawk. Kanti recognized her from before. He noticed that she was chasing Eek down, grasping him in her talons and flying off, low at first as he was quite a load for her, so she landed nearby to finish the job, and finish the job she did. Eek was no more. This gave Sleg a diversion. He had noticed the door of the Pine Stone Inn. He scrambled over to it and started banging.

"Open up you vermin! You will grant me entry, or I will kill any animal I find whether they are crawling, scrambling, or slithering!"

"I will not!" bellowed Wuchak from within.

Just then Apitah landed on a boulder behind Sleg. Sleg spun around hissing and snapping his teeth.

"You! You are next! You sky-devil!" He rushed at Apitah, screeching, and screaming with rage.

Apitah lifted off into the air with little effort as Sleg lunged. His weight was more than he could control. He fell flat his belly, on the boulder. Apitah came back down on his back, talons first. The scream from Sleg echoed through the clearing, through the forest, and through the thick stone walls of the Pine Stone Inn. Apitah's talons sunk into Sleg's back, and with his beak, he gripped the back of Sleg's neck and finished him. The reign of Sleg–Sleg the selfish–Sleg the sinister–Sleg the slaughterer, was over.

"Let him be, Apitah. He would not be good to eat." Kanti had landed in time to see the end. "Carry him to the river and drop him in."

"Another kind of hawk took that other rat," reported Apitah.

"Yes, I know her. I trust that she is now headed back downriver and not hunting here. She did us a service," Kanti replied.

"The others?" asked Apitah.

"I got one of them. The other two fled. With all those who hunt in the canyon now out looking for rats, they should not get far."

Apitah looks down at the lifeless Sleg. "I shall drop this one off in the river and return to my kind. I can see them soaring far above us."

"I thought I had the gift of eyesight. You, my dear friend, can see forever. Thank you for your bravery and your talons... I mean talents."

Apitah nodded quickly. "Next stop, the river." He flew off with the remains of Sleg in his grasp.

Kanti wrapped on the door of the Pine Stone Inn.

"Wuchak! It is Kanti. Can you open the door? The enemy is slain."

The little door in the upper portion of the heavy wooden door opened, only this time, there was no nose sniffing the air, or eye rolling around in the opening.

"Kanti? Is that you?"

"Yes, is that you?" came the raven's reply.

"Tis I Wuchak. I want to stand back, do ya know. Cannot tell who is on the other side, eye... nose 'n all."

"Well, are you going to let me in?"

"Oh, for certain, Mr. Kanti. It will not be but a second."

The little door slammed shut and the old familiar sound of wooden beams being slid aside could be heard. Wuchak opened the door, but before Kanti could step in, Wuchak jutted his head through the doorway and looked first left and then right.

"May I come in now?"

"Oh, yes, yes Mr. Kanti, come right in. Cannot be too careful, can we?"

"No, we cannot. Bring me a bowl of pine nut brew, will you?"

"Straight away, straight away."

"I would like a nice quiet place to sip it, so I can think."

"As you wish. I should tell you that you are the fellow everyone says was the hero that saved Rimrock... and uh, I would just like to say thank you, to you and yours for doin' it."

"Many, braver than I, defended Rimrock last night."

"I will not be listnin ta any of that there modesty, Mr. Kanti. I was there at the gatherin too, ya know."

"Well, thank you, my friend. We all came together. Something tells me we will have more to do. Much more. Now, how about that pine nut brew?"

"Comin' right up!" Wuchak returned quickly with Kanti's cup of pine nut brew.

He dipped his bill in silence and thought of the night before. How can nice innocent folk like the villagers of Rimrock see such things and not be changed? His mind drifted back to a time when he was younger. He missed his mate. She and all the eggs had fallen with a tree, cut down to make room for humans. Before that were happy days when he could look forward with a breezy way of seeing things. As is the way of nature, it recovers quickly and moves on, repairing damage, and so must he. Some things trigger memories though, and that is what makes us who we are.

"Kanti? Kanti?"

Pulled from his thoughts, Kanti looked up to see a towel and an enormous apron. Wuchak had returned to check on him.

"Are you all right, Mr. Kanti? Would you like more?"

"No. Normally, Wuchak, that would be a fine idea. But today, I must fly back to Rimrock."

THE BRIGHT LIGHT OF A
NEW DAY

Teek returned to Stonewood Place to find it filled with villagers. Some of them had never seen the inside of this well-known home.

"Teek, our village is no longer safe. Everyone now knows of our location. Nothing will ever be the same as it was. How are we to remain safe, from humans, from predators, from birds, what do we do now?" asked Pinion, Cheek's papa.

"Sir, things will definitely never be the same," Teek confirmed. "Rimrock has become known to everyone. All creatures. We also have many allies we did not have before. We must face a new day. There are much bigger problems that we now need to address. We are all in this together. The bright light of day is now brighter. Let us now go and greet it."

"We do not want your adventurous life here. We were perfectly fine before all of this."

"You were not fine, you only thought you were. You cannot continue as you have been, hiding in your burrows, never venturing from the village, thinking only of your own comfort. We share this canyon with many animals, and if it had not been for them, and the help of humans, we might have lost Rimrock forever. Some of those animals died fighting for you last night! Now follow me out into a new bright light. We are now safe because of the help of others. We will help them when their time comes."

"Seek? Are you going to let this stand?"

"I am. He is right. You might not be standing here right now, Pinion, if it had not been for the gathering, the ancient human, the help of our friends out there sitting in our grassy area, the other animals that fought to save Rimrock, some were killed. This is a brave new world, whether you like that or not. The time of privilege and entitlement is over."

It seemed that the entire village poured out of Stonewood Place. Out they filed, young, old, female, male, all starting and stopping, sniffing the air, looking up to the top of the rimrock walls as if there may be someone or something peering down at them.

⁕❋⁕

"I've never seen you this way, Sofia," said Nute.

"To be honest, neither have I," added Walter.

Walter put his arm around his granddaughter. Nute sat in front of her cross-legged and held her hand.

"During times such as these," Nute said, "it is best to begin to think of all those that you have helped save and all that has been preserved. We did the work of Ipsusnute last night. I am sure that he is proud."

"I should not have expected you to participate in such a messy business, Sofia. That was not easy for any of us. So much killing and death is a sacrifice some make, but it is not they that cause it. It is the evil they face that causes it. That evil must be met aggressively, bravely, with force and strength, not weakness and avoidance. But this is most definitely not for everyone, just as many people cannot be farmers or doctors. These things require some very unpleasant, yet necessary tasks. I made a mistake by not explaining this to you. We all found ourselves caught up in this, not knowing the extent of it."

"I think it was glorious!" It was Tap, back from the front line. He felt most invigorated, excited, and proud. He seemed to lift his eight legs a little higher as he walked. He was not meant to wait or retreat, he wanted to face danger head-on, and so he had.

"Well, that certainly is another way of looking at it, I suppose," Kanti's voice came from overhead.

Fwoop, fwoop, fwoop, fwoop. Kanti landed. "I think I am getting the hang of dropping down into this village between the rimrock. How is everyone?"

Walter answered, "That depends upon of whom you speak."

"What is that. Old English?" It was Sofia.

"Ah, I think she may be rallying. She's back. This will all be just a memory now, and that is something that we can work through."

"Tap! You are well? Where did you go?" Digger approached the group in the central grassy area, being one of the first to emerge from the Stonewood Place burrow.

"I think I may be able to answer that for him," said Kanti. "Tap, this new and courageous friend of yours, was nothing short of heroic. I saw no less than twelve rats at a time, charge toward the edge of the cliff and fall to the rocks below. I landed to try to figure out the cause. It is then that I noticed this little fellow hopping out from under a boulder. I heard him say *that ought to take care of those mangy vermin!* I asked him if that whole thing was caused by him, and he answered me by saying that it was a simple trick of deception. He may be small, but he has a huge and courageous heart!"

"That deception took care of no less than 125 rats!" claimed a proud Tap.

Digger was impressed. "This way, Tap! Come over to the other side of the creek with me, in front of Stonewood Place. I want you to meet some of the villagers you helped." Tap had gained respect and found a new admirer in Digger.

Teek scampered up to the group, bringing with him Cicci, Peeps, and Digger. Walter and Nute were still comforting Sofia. Walter looked over to Teek, smiled, and raised his eyebrows.

"Sofia, I would like to thank you for protecting us as you did," said Teek.

"Yes," added Cicci, "Thank you. You were very brave."

Teek turned to Nute. "Nute, I have been pondering something that

I think is important, that you may be very interested in. It could be a good way to move forward from this dreadful event. I can show you the resting place of your ancestor. I know where he lies, and it is not far from here. If we squirrels rode on your shoulders, we could make it there and back rather quickly. Walter, I do remember you saying that you would like to see this place, but it is not a place for you now."

"I am perfectly fine waiting for you here in the village. That journey would be too much for me, and actually, I believe I shall be quite comfortable in this spot. I'm out of the sun, there is plenty of fresh water, I have this blanket, and I have Seek here to keep me company. We can discuss the future of Rimrock. I am most fortunate to be here with all of you. Now listen though, be careful. I don't want to add a rescue effort to all of this."

"All right, well the rest of us will..."

"Teek?"

"Yes, Peeps?"

"My momma needs me here right now. I think I would like to stay behind as well."

"Yes, good idea. She needs you right now."

"Teek?"

"Yes, Digger?"

"I was thinking of exploring the tunnels behind your wall, and I can sort of show Tap around a bit. Is that all right?"

"Yes, Digger, that is fine." Teek looked over at Walter, saying in a low voice, "Must have been the words 'rescue effort.' So... Nute, Sofia, Cicci? We do have time, but we should get started if we are to make it back before the bright light of day is down. Is this something you want to do?"

They all nodded.

"Alright then, let us get started. The location is downriver from here."

"Sofia, can you carry us? It will be a lot faster, and safer that way."

"Grandpa, are you sure it is okay for me to leave you here?"

"I am absolutely sure, sweetie. I will probably take a nap; I am very comfortable where I am, and I am very tired after last night. You go on. I'll be fine. I'll be right here when you get back. This spot is as comfortable as my easy chair. We made sandwiches and brought other treats. I have everything I need. Make sure you take some with you."

"Sofia, may Cicci and I ride on your shoulders again?"

"Hop on! I'm ready!"

Kanti was still concerned about the conditions outside the walls of Rimrock, saying, "Allow me to go see how the cleanup is going and make sure that you are safe to travel before you leave these protective walls."

Teek responded. "None of us have seen outside since the fighting began, except maybe Tap. I appreciate your protection, especially since it means the safety of Cicci and others, but Kanti, you do know that my little group has been through many dangerous situations. We are alright for travel. We are riding on humans. I do realize that you have been to our rescue on many occasions, but I think we will make it there and back safely."

But Kanti persisted. "Then trust me and heed my caution on this occasion. A lot has gone on out there that is dangerous. One of those predators that protected your village last night might mistake you for a rat. No little ones, I should go look first. There were things out there that some of you should not see... things that many creatures wish they had not seen. Although you are riding on the shoulders of humans, the burial chamber is still downriver from the Pine Stone Inn. That is a bit of a journey. Also, at this time, we do not know the whereabouts of Dennis Digwood, or what he might be up to. Ipsusnute took away his killing stick, but he *is* unpredictable, dangerous, and still out there somewhere. I understand the need to be outside of these walls, and I know that we need to keep moving forward and choose the way of action. So, just wait for my return, I will not be long at all. Then I will tell you if it is alright for you to journey to the chamber."

The discussion was made, and the discussion was over. Kanti was right, and he was their most trusted counsel. With those words, he flew off. He landed on a branch above three coyotes trotting around with their noses to the ground.

Kanti called to them. "From what I see from above, I do not think that there is anything left here for you."

"What went on here, raven? We smell it."

"Last night, much happened. Today, nothing is happening."

"We came from over past the round mountain," one of the coyotes said, "over that way." She pointed her nose east, toward the high desert. "We heard the birds spreading news of this. Have we come too late?"

"That all depends on what you are here for. Maybe not too late for a meal. There are animals that live here in the canyon that are still cleaning up. But be warned, this is not your territory, there may be other packs of coyotes and other creatures that will aggressively defend this canyon from outsiders. Mind you, we could use scavengers and hunters like you right now, there is much to do. There is also much here that you do not know. The creatures of this canyon no longer consider ground squirrels to be prey."

The three coyotes looked at each other knowingly.

Kanti could see that they did not take his words seriously, and so he added, "If you hunt ground squirrels, you too will be hunted. As I said, there is more going on here than I have told you but heed my words."

"We will heed your words, raven, and we will keep our ears and noses on alert."

Downriver, there may be many that have floated to the banks and other shores or have been caught by boulders or branches. Follow your noses, they should lead you in the right direction."

The coyotes looked at each other to see if they all agreed, circling around each other, yipping, and nipping, as packs do, then replied.

"Then we shall be on our way, raven. We will travel downriver as you say. What *are* prey animals eating? What is this all about? Our noses tell us that there has been much fighting and death here, only a short while ago."

"Rats. You smell rats," replied Kanti.

"Rats? What are rats?"

"They are a grey rodent, a mouse-like creature, only much larger, and when in packs, seem quite aggressive and even violent. They are not from around here. The ones that were here were attacking us. They are now dead or have scattered. I hope you find them. The reason they were here is because humans brought them. Humans are the reason you hide during the day and travel at night. Humans carry killing sticks."

"We know. One of them killed one of my pups with a killing stick."

"So, you know how unpredictable and dangerous they are. A great loss, I am sure. If you find one of these rats, you will know what all rats are. It will look and smell like the rest. They are much larger than the rodents you normally hunt, but they are tough and taste odd."

The three coyotes looked at each other and headed down the path leading downriver, trotting faster than before. Satisfied for the moment that the squirrels would be safe on the shoulders of humans, Kanti waited and watched the coyotes disappear, then lifted off, and headed back to Rimrock.

Fwoop, fwoop, fwoop. Kanti landed on a boulder halfway up the cliff overlooking Rimrock. Sofia and Nute were ready for travel. Sofia had Teek and Cicci on her shoulders, and they were making sure that Walter was comfortable.

"Well? May we depart?" Sofia asked.

"There are still predators, some of them are not from our canyon, they come from another territory. So, there is still some danger. But most everything has been carried away or consumed."

Nute spoke, gazing into the sky. "That is the way of things like this... that is why everything always looks so clean out here in the canyon. There is a provision for everything in nature. Everything is cleaned and utilized. It is nature's way."

"Not like where the humans live," added Kanti.

"Not all humans, Kanti. Not these humans," said Teek.

"You are right, not all humans."

"Most of them though... there are too many of them." Walter added. He had been laying back with his eyes close, but he had been listening.

"I will meet you at the entrance. From there I will fly ahead and bring back any word of possible danger or difficulty."

Sofia checked in on Walter one last time, and they were off. They headed out through the passage, they looked forward to seeing the river and being on the trail once again. Halfway through the passage, they came upon a couple of remaining dead rats.

"Look at their faces," Cicci observed.

Everyone looked closer.

"Do you see how terrified they are? It is almost as if they died of fright!"

Nute knelt and examined them closely, then lifted his face toward the walls of the passage.

"They were dashed against the rock walls, that is what killed them, then they fell here. But they did see something that frightened them. They were surprised and yes, quite frightened."

"What was it Nute?"

"Dunno, exactly, but I would say that these are some pretty big human-type footprints. But much bigger than human."

There was silence among them. Hair and fur seemed to stand on end.

Sofia spoke quietly. "Nute, can you go back and let the guard squirrels know? We will wait here... hurry."

Nute sprang into action and returned quickly. They then continued toward the opening in the cliffs. They arrived at the entrance to find Kanti waiting for them.

"How is it so far?"

"No major difficulties, a couple of dead rats back there... and some tracks," Nute answered.

"Tracks? What kind of tracks?"

"I'm not sure, but whatever it was, it appears that the rats were quite frightened when they died."

"It must have been an ambush."

"I suppose so."

"Do the guard squirrels know?"

"Yes."

"Alright then, away you go."

2 2

ANCESTRAL REUNION

No humans have an animal's ability to smell and sense a story. This is how they receive news, hunt, and survive. There was something about the surrounding area that hung in the air. Teek, Cicci, Sofia, and Nute stopped and looked around. They could hear and feel the dry wind blowing the sandy soil. They noticed thousands of paw prints and scuffles that would soon be gone, blown away by winds flowing through the canyon.

For now, the ground still showed clear signs of a fight, the trampling of grass and small plants, tufts of fur, some still attached to hide. In some places, teeth and claws lay in the sandy soil. In other places, there were what looked like dried black pools.

"It would be best if you keep moving, and not look too closely." Kanti was perched on the top of a boulder in front of them.

They moved on without a word. He watched them pass, then lifted off. No one said anything for some time. They were all deep in quiet reflection.

Finally, Sofia spoke, mostly to break the silence. "It is going to be a hot summer."

"Yes, I think so," Nute replied. "It seems hot already, rather early for that."

They chose a seldom-used deer path close to the bank of the river, pushing through thick brush. They decided not to choose the easiest path, but they felt that it might be the safest. Every so often they would stop to rest. This gave them a chance to look around and notice signs of activity.

"Look over there, Cicci," said Teek, "up the hill, between those two rocks. More dead rats... and over there. What is that? It is bigger."

"We should not go look. I will be glad when this is all gone," she replied.

"We must remember this, so it is never repeated," added Sofia.

Nute walked back to where Teek and Cicci sat atop Sofia's shoulders. "My people still speak of our history and the trouble we have been through. We will not forget. You shouldn't either. These experiences make you who you are."

Fwoop, fwoop, fwoop. Kanti landed and called quietly to the group.

"Quiulup, I have spotted Dennis Digwood just around the bend. Ipsusnute, maybe you can venture close enough to see where he is and what he is doing. The rest of you, no sound, not even the sound of branches or twigs! Watch me. If I hold up a wing, you stop."

Nute moved forward making no sound and peered carefully around a basalt cliff jutting out closer to the bank of the river.

Dennis Digwood seemed to be focusing on an area of ground near his feet. He was moving his arm as if tossing something out in front of him, yet strangely, he was not tossing anything. Nute could just make out what he said.

"C'mon, here you go, that's it. Ha! You thought I had something for you. Used to being fed, aren't you? You are easily fooled. I guess you're not very bright after all. That's right, I understand your little squeaks. Confused? You should be. Now tell me what I need to know, or I'll poison all of you! Come back here!"

Nute could see small ground squirrels scattering and running back up the hill into their hiding places. Ditching was always the most common response to danger for all squirrels. They knew every hole, crack, and rock in their area, and could find them quickly.

Nute returned and whispered to the others, "He is busy scrambling up the hill trying to fool some local ground squirrels and press them for information. I think if we keep low and stay on this path, he will not notice us."

Kanti acknowledged, saying in his most quiet voice, which was not at all what he was used to, "When you are ready, I will fly further up the hill and out of sight, in case he has found another killing stick, there I will make my usual calls, this will let you know that you can move past. Is everyone alright with that?"

They all nodded.

"Sit behind my head so you don't get smacked with branches, we need to hide behind these willows and stoop low as we go," Sofia directed.

Kanti flew low and well away from Dennis Digwood and up to the top of the rimrock. There he began to croak at the top of his lungs.

"That's it, let's go," Sofia whispered.

Nute placed his pointer finger over his mouth and then motioned to them to follow. They walked below Dennis, under the brush without a sound.

They could hear Dennis sputtering and muttering course language in frustration about an old "crow" scaring away the squirrels. It was not the croaking raven but his own scrambling and nasty noises that scattered the squirrels.

Teek, Cicci, Sofia, Nute, hiked silently past Dennis Digwood completely undetected. They didn't stop until they were around another bend and out of sight and earshot. Kanti was already there to meet them, greet them, and compliment them. At the same time, Dennis Digwood needed to regroup. He had found his ride out of the canyon.

"Get me outta here!" Bill had shown up looking for Dennis at his sister's pleading. Like it or not, Trisha was still Dennis' wife and so, still showed concern for his well-being.

"Home or office?"

"Anywhere but here! Home, I guess!"

They sped off without Bill uttering a word, until Dennis asked him a direct question. "Have you seen Ricky?"

"I have not."

"Tell him he's fired. Did he return the truck?"

"Yes, I believe he did," replied Bill.

"Good. Otherwise, I'd send the police after him. We need to find someone I can depend on! I'm surrounded by idiots!"

⁕ ⁕ ⁕

Around the bend, on the other side of the rock cliff, Kanti landed and made an announcement. "Dennis Digwood has left the canyon... for now. I was able to fly away as he was reaching the top. Someone came to get him, riding in one of those fast beasts. He really stomped out of here, up the hill. He did not seem very happy."

Nute spoke-up. "Well, if he ever leaves here happy, you let me know and I will change that in a hurry!"

Sofia stared at Nute. This was a side of him that she had not seen before. Not the quiet gentle soul she was familiar with. It was a good side to see and Nute saw support in the expression on Sofia's squinting, smiling face. She punched him in the shoulder, a sign of approval.

"One thing is quite unknown to me, how is it that a person such as he can communicate with the animals of the canyon? I must find this answer. There is more to this than we know. You are almost to your destination. The boulder slide is just ahead. Ipsusnute, you and Sofia must search for an entrance. The rest of us will find a protected place and I will keep a watch out."

"It is a wonder that this boulder slide didn't destroy the burial chamber." Sofia looked out across a vast hillside of large basalt boulders.

"He didn't want the land slide to destroy the burial chamber," she said wistfully. "He just wanted it covered up, so that it could not be found by other humans. He wanted his beloved ground squirrels to find him."

"Where do we begin to search for the opening?" asked Teek.

"This may take a while. I am not sure that we can figure this out and get back to Rimrock. Sofia, I do know that you want to discover this with me, but..."

"You're right." She knew what came next, and so wanted it to be her words. "I should return and get grandpa home."

"Come back tomorrow," said Nute, "I will still be here. Maybe by then, I'll know a way inside."

"We were able to find our way into the burial chamber by a drum beat and I felt like I was being called or pulled. Maybe I can help you." Teek then turned to Cicci. He did not need to speak.

"I shall return here with Sofia tomorrow. You two be very careful. If you start moving boulders, you could start the whole moving down the hill again and there would be nobody to help you."

Kanti spoke. "I will stay also, but I do not venture underground. It is best that I keep watch out here."

Teek and Cicci touched their noses in a few moments of silent tender departure.

"You be careful. This is not worth risking your lives for. This might take more time. Come back to me." She told him.

"You know I will."

Nute moved close to Sofia so that Teek could climb onto his shoulder. He looked into Sofia's eyes.

"Perhaps we will touch noses one day..."

"Perhaps," she replied.

Teek's eyes widened as he looked over at Cicci. She returned his look with a knowing smile. Decisions and goodbyes concluded, they parted.

"I would like to fly over them for a little way. Then I will return. Maybe you can just take a look around, then when I return, if you have found a way in, I will be here to see where the opening is."

"Thank you, Kanti."

"Then once you make it into the burial chamber, you can bring me one of those golden shiny things you spoke of, Teek."

"Agreed. Kanti, there is no one more deserving than you."

Kanti flew after Sofia and Cicci. Nute stood before the large slope of boulders. Teek sat on his shoulder. The bright light of day beat down directly overhead. The air was completely still. The sun was hot enough to make the plants perspire, giving off fragrances.

"Do you hear that?" asked Nute.

"No, what?" asked Teek.

"Neither do I. There is no sound. I do not hear birds. The wind is also still. I can just barely hear the distant roar of rapids, but even that seems very quiet."

They continued to examine the boulders before them with their eyes, looking for any sign, anything that might stand out as being different. From where they stood, there was nothing.

"We do not need to stay in this spot you know," Teek finally mentioned. "Maybe we will see something from another position?"

They moved a little higher up the hill. New facets showed themselves to the visitors. Still no sign.

"Somewhere under all those boulders is your ancestor. The ancient human, the spirit that looks out over this canyon. Oh, you should have been at the gathering, Ipsusnute. I would have wanted you to be there. Your ancestor appeared to the creatures of the canyon. He showed himself and set a beam that changed us so that we could all join to help each other. It was a moment like never before. And here we are now. It is good that you are here now. A great cycle has come back to us, this is how things happen in this world, reoccurring events, it is not– like this happens and then that happens, in a line, as humans think, the nature of this world is a cycle. It is light, then it is dark, and then it is light again. Everything comes back. It is hot now, then it will be cold, and the sky will turn white and fall to the ground, then it will become warm again and turn back into water. We sleep and then we are awake. It is the way of things."

"This is also the way of my people. We are different humans. We are part of the natural world. We do not try to fight it or control it. This world gives us life, and we are grateful. We know this to be true."

"Look there, Ipsusnute! Just up the hill there. There is another flat place. It looks almost as though the path is..."

"Those are steps."

"Steps?"

"Made by humans to help walk to that spot. They are made to match my steps. Hang on."

Nute climbed the ancient and somewhat crumbled steps, reaching the flat spot, they began to quietly view the boulders before them.

"There, there! There it is. Do you hear that?"

"I do not. At least, I don't think so... I do feel a little cooler though. There is something cool coming from the boulders. It comes from over there."

They both turned to look to their left, just slightly downhill. Off to one side of the landing, they stood on more crumbled steps that disappeared between two enormous boulders. These two boulders were decidedly larger than all the rest. Ipsusnute took a step down.

"You should wait for Kanti to return."

"I'm just getting a little closer to see what I can see, that's all. Look there!"

On one of the faces of one of the large boulders was a marking, a red spiral pictograph.

Between the two large boulders, the steps disappeared into the darkness.

"I think I may be able to fit through there. Where is Kanti?" asked Nute.

"I am up here. *Kkkkkk.*"

Above them, on top of one of the two large boulders, Kanti landed.

"I have been above, on, or near this boulder field many times. But I have never seen this opening, or this pictograph, until now. I wonder if it can be seen from any angle but the one you found there on that flat area behind you. My guess is no, or I would have seen it. I will stay above ground here while you go down, there. *Quiulup*, as you know, I am not much for the underground. I do go visit Ahtūnowhiho sometimes, but I would much rather be flying above than crawling below. I might go perch in the tree over there instead of out here baking in the sun, but I will still be here watching and listening."

"All right, in we go," said Nute.

"Nute, would it help you for me to go first to scout the way, then you follow when I let you know of the way ahead?

"Stick close to me, Teek. I think I'd rather you be near me."

"I think that sounds better too," Teek replied. They both peered down into the darkness.

They stood in the entrance feeling the cool airflow from below. The silence was broken by Teek's quiet voice. "Listen. Can you hear it?"

Nute stood frozen, staring at Teek. "I do hear it. The distant drum calls to us. It beckons to us to come closer."

"That is the sign that the ancient human awaits us. Are you ready?"

Nute took a deep breath and nodded. "I will need to feel my way through, it is too dark for me to see."

"As we get nearer the burial chamber, I do remember there being an unexplainable golden light, it may have been the illumination stones. When we get closer, I think your way will become illuminated."

"I will need to go slow to make sure I have good footing, probably slower than you are used to."

"We will stay together," agreed Teek.

Nute stepped down slowly with his hands on the walls. Over the eons, the boulders had shifted and slide closer together. This made squeezing through the descending passage not only difficult for Nute, but quite unnerving.

"Are you still with me?"

"I made it through. At least we won't get turned around. Out is up."

There was a bit of silence while Teek pondered how anyone could get turned around underground. Teek finally replied with a simple, "This way."

The going was slow, and the footing was unsure. Every so often

Nute would call out to Teek in the darkness. Teek stayed close to him, realizing that his reply was the assurance of the way forward. The drumbeats became louder and were now accompanied by strange windy whispers.

"Teek, I think I am hearing whispers. I hear my name. *Ipsusnute, I await you*, it says."

"You understand what the whispers are saying?"

"Yes, it is the language of my people. I hear the words whispered in my ear. Do you hear it?"

"Maybe it is just meant for you. Follow me. Once around this bend, the passageway will be lighter, and you should be able to see much more."

The passage continued to descend, but now it made a sharp turn to the left, the downhill side. As it did, Nute could see the wall of stone in front of them. It was lit by a warm light that revealed a reddish pictograph of a human figure, holding something in its hand.

"Is that him?" asked Nute.

"Yes," replied Teek.

"Ipsusnute?"

"Yes."

"What is he holding?" asked Nute.

"An Illumination Stone."

"Can I see him now?"

"You seem to be shivering a bit. How do you feel?"

"I am cold. Very cold."

"Yes. It was cold before. I do not know why." The squirrel looked up at the human. "Nute, I would like to prepare you. You may find the remains of your ancestor a little difficult to see. Nothing remains of him but his bones. There are many wondrous things in there with him, but make no mistake, this *is* where he lies."

"I understand what this is. I am ready."

"All right then. Follow me."

Teek moved down the passageway toward the chamber looking back over his shoulder to make sure that Nute was following him. This passageway entered the chamber behind where the ancient human sat.

They both stopped in the entrance to the chamber to take it all in. The drumbeats and the whispering stopped suddenly. Teek looked out into the large, vaulted chamber. He looked up at Nute.

"Something is different."

"What is different?" asked Nute.

"He looks different from over here. All I can see are the things that covered him."

Nute stared in the direction of his ancestor. "Where is Ipsusnute? He is gone! I see his clothing but there are no remains!"

Teek had no words to offer. The ancient human was gone.

"How could this be?" said Nute. "Has someone taken him? If that were the case, then surely there are far more valuable artifacts than his bones that they could have removed. But there it all still is! This chamber holds the story of my people. Oh, if only the elders could see this!"

Teek and Nute looked out over the same artifacts that Teek had seen before.

The enormous, vaulted chamber, in addition to the glowing and bedazzling Illumination Stones, still held some very familiar artifacts. Nute recognized bows, arrows, and spears made of obsidian and jasper, the beaded cords and woven leather ropes hanging on bone hooks, pottery that had held grain for his journey to the spirit world, necklaces of beads, claws, teeth, and feathers, and beautifully woven baskets full to overflowing with gold. Some of the gold was in nugget form, some flattened into coins. All these artifacts lay there untouched, all untouched but the ancient human himself.

"As you can see, Nute, this chamber, and your ancestor, was the source of our precious and mysterious Illumination Stone. All of this represents an age long past, now just a quiet whisper in our ears."

Teek and Nute focused their attention on where the ancient human had laid. His clothing and vestments still lay in exactly the same arrangement they would have been, had he been wearing them. His elk skin, moccasins, eagle and hawk feather headdress, headband was lined with gems. They were all still there, right down to his breastplate of buffalo bone, and beaded tassels, but *he* was not.

"There is something else," whispered Teek.

"Yes?"

"He held a wooden staff. I touched it and went way up. Now it is also gone!"

"You went up?"

"Yes, above the canyon. I met him there. That is when I realized who he was and first felt the power that surrounds us."

Teek realized that things had gotten suddenly quiet, so he looked up at Nute. Nute looked straight ahead, his eyes fixed and unblinking. Teek followed his gaze.

There, standing at the other side of the chamber was the ancient human, Ipsusnute. It was as though he were alive. He appeared as though he were solid flesh and bone, and fully alive. In his hand, he held the ceremonial staff. He held it out as if to present it to them. On it, they could clearly see the same symbolic images as the pictographs.

"Ipsusnute? Ipsusnute? Do you see him, too?"

The ancient human spoke first, he spoke Sahaptian, the native tongue of Nimipuu, saying, "Tá'c 'ee páayn: It is good you came."

Nute opened his mouth, the words he spoke were also Sahaptian, words that Teek could somehow understand. Nute replied to his ancient ancestor with, "Qe'ciyew'yew: Thank you."

The ancient human, fully manifested before them and wearing his magnificent ceremonial adornments, radiated a colorful undulating light that enveloped him and illuminated the entire chamber. Nute stood as if in a trance, his unblinking stare peering through the great veil of life into another dimension.

Teek backed up, overwhelmed by the presence and power of Ipsusnute. Ipsusnute turned his gaze, smiling and radiating a deep caring and kindness for him. Teek felt enveloped with the warmth and love that let him know that he was protected and important.

Nute and his ancestor continued their exchange. Nute mostly listened and would only respond to acknowledge the words spoken to him.

Teek remembered Kanti's request, and so began to ask, "May I?..."

"You may bring Kanti his request." Ipsusnute, the ancient one, already knew Teek's intention, gr anted Teek's request. Teek took one gold piece from a basket. Nute then heard the words of Ipsusnute in his mind.

"Long ago, I brought Illumination to Rimrock and other creatures of the canyon. Now the world is not as it was. Evil is among us. The canyon and all its creatures are in great danger. Those you trust have brought you here now to help you manifest my energy. You and these brave creatures have a great struggle before you with those that have come to destroy you. You and those you trust will save this canyon from the evil that has arrived to occupy it.

There is a great force below. It is earth's way of creating land but only the small creatures who dwell underground can access its power. Only they can find the way to use it. Ahtūnowhiho will help them find what they need."

The ancient human paused but continued when Nute nodded. "All your times have come. You must now protect your world. You and those you trust will save this canyon from the evil that has arrived to occupy it. The day is coming when there will be nothing again. That will be a good day, not created by evil."

Ipsusnute extended his ceremonial staff, handing it to Nute. The staff entered the physical world.

"I give you my ceremonial staff, Ipsusnute. Take it and know that you may use it to summon me. You are now my connection to this world. Trust those that are close to you. Match the beat of the drum by tapping the staff on a stone three times and say my name. Follow your heart. I will be with you to guide your way. Prepare yourselves for the great conflict ahead."

Teek and Nute glanced at each other, Nute held the ceremonial staff in disbelief. When they glanced back, the ancient human, Ipsusnute, was gone.

"What now?" asked Nute.

"I guess we leave," Teek guessed.

"I now have the ceremonial staff. Should I see if it works?"

Teek thought for a moment, "Maybe not yet," he concluded. "It is probably best to use it when you really need him. This way, follow me."

Teek began to bound back up the stone steps to the entrance. Nute felt the stone walls as he ascended, until the daylight, now late afternoon, illuminated the steps in front of him. Once outside, they both examined the staff carefully.

"You should probably keep this with you at all times... and keep it in a safe place when you are elsewhere." Teek said.

Nute nodded. "The safest place I can think of is Rimrock. When I am elsewhere, it should be kept at Rimrock."

"Well?" An impatient raven waited for them when they exited the cavern.

"We saw him as if he were in the flesh, Kanti!" Teek still couldn't believe it.

"Is that a ceremonial staff? Did he give that to you, Ipsusnute?"

"He did."

"Then you may call upon him from this moment on. Teek, did you bring me what I asked?"

"I did. I gave it to Nute to carry."

Nute pulled the gold piece from his pocket and held it up. Kanti soared to the top of one of the large, tall boulders where they stood. Nute reached out with the gold piece and presented it to Kanti. Kanti reached out with his beak and grabbed it. "It is a wondrous thing. I shall place this in the center of my nest."

"You have a nest? Where *is* your nest?" Teek asked.

Kanti was caught off-guard by this question. He had let it slip that he had a nest, and now it was time for back-peddling.

"Oh, it is really nothing. Small and insignificant. Quite some distance from here actually... So, are you ready to head back to Rimrock? I will fly on ahead and make sure everything is safe."

With that, he flew off with the gold piece in his beak. Once out of sight of Teek and Nute, he took a detour toward his nest for a quick deposit.

"I would not use that ceremonial staff as a walking stick. Who is to say that the third time you place it on the ground you wouldn't initiate your ancestor to appear?"

"I'd have to say his name."

"Oh, yes, that is right." Teek had already forgotten that.

"Still, I should carry it, not use it to walk."

"You should carry me as well. It will make the going a lot faster. What if you walked back to Rimrock by way of the trail above the ridge instead of down by the river? Where has Kanti flown off to?"

"You have many ideas to offer, Teek."

"Well, I am sitting right next to your ear, I may as well. I hope that Sofia and Walter are still at Rimrock so I can say goodbye."

<hr>

"Sofia, Cicci, you are back already. Where's Teek and Nute?" Walter was having a relaxing conversation with Seek when Sofia and Cicci entered the village. Their attention immediately switched as Sofia sat down and Cicci scampered off to take a position next to her on the grass. Sofia sat in front of her grandpa. "There was no telling how long it was going to take to find an entrance large enough for a human to enter, so we felt it was best for the two of us to return. I can see that you get home and that you are well and comfortable."

"So, Teek and Nute are still at the burial chamber?" asked Seek.

"Yes. They may be a while," replied Cicci.

"Seek and I were discussing the idea of having a special gathering of our own, right here in the central grassy area, only this would not be like one of those colony story-telling nights. This would be during the day and be a special event that would require the participation of the villagers. Any questions, suggestions, or ideas that anyone has can be contributed."

"I like that idea. Get all the villagers to agree on where we go from here," Cicci concluded.

"It is also better to hold it out here in the central grassy area so that we can include Kanti and possibly you humans. Our concerns have become further reaching than this secluded colony, and the inside of this canyon." Seek reasoned.

"Our recent journey made that very clear to us," added Cicci.

"Let me help you up, Grandpa, you've been sitting there for quite a while." Sofia put her arm around Walter to help him up.

"Where's my cane? Seek, I'd like to return to attend that colony gathering if I may. Sofie can let me know."

"By all means! We look forward to your wise counsel."

Cicci looked up at the humans. "Sofia, I think I had better go now to Stonewood Place, or behind the walls of Stonewood place, to see if anyone needs my help finding their way home. So, I shall say farewell, until I see you again... come back soon."

Sofia nodded. "We will see you soon. C'mon, Grandpa, let me help you through the passage and back up the hill."

⁂

Teek and Nute, having emerged from the burial chamber, were climbing the hill up to the boulder mound that held the Pine Stone Inn.

"It is getting late; they may have already left so that Sofia can get Walter back home," Teek noted.

As they ascended the hill up toward the upper trail, Teek heard humans talking.

"Ipsusnute!" Nute turned quickly in the direction of Teek, sitting on his shoulder. "I hear human voices and see movement up ahead!"

Nute quickly hid behind a tree and slowly peeked around, but he could not identify the people. They waited. Soon the people came closer, stepped out into a clearing. It was Sofia and Walter!

"Good fortune indeed," exclaimed Teek. "Walter! Sofia! Let me down please Nute."

Nute could barely stoop quickly enough before Teek had hopped off and was scrambling toward Walter and Sofia.

Sofia was first to notice them and called out. "Did you see him?" she asked.

Teek told Walter and Sofia the whole story, from the missing bones and appearance of Ipsusnute to the gold piece awarded to Kanti. Nute handed the ceremonial staff to Walter for him to examine.

"I have been gifted with this by my ancestor. It is much like one of your tapping sticks, only there is more on it," he said.

"Yes, Nute, it is the staff of Ipsusnute. It is a connection between this world and the next."

"Ipsusnute is among us." It was Kanti, just above them on a branch.

"I knew there was something special about you," Sofia said as she hugged Nute. Walter winked.

NO COINCIDENCE

"Rough day?"

"You could say that."

Ricky Harvey sat facing the older woman behind the enormous and elaborately carved, wooden tavern counter. With one hand holding up his chin, and the other grasping his beverage, his face was defeated, holding a "what now" expression.

"I think I lost my job today."

"Oh? Where did you work?"

"I worked at Digwood Development."

"Dennis Digwood?"

"Yup."

"Well then, this one's on me, you can celebrate! I know Digwood. He deceived me and manipulated me. Now he has my land. I now work here to make ends meet." She reached out, offering a handshake. "Hi. My name is Gladys Ainsley."

"Ricky Harvey," he said, greeting her in return.

"This is the first day of the rest of your life, Ricky! Good riddance, I say. Do you know what I also say? 'When one door closes, another door opens.' Sometimes a new door can't open until the other one closes, and sometimes that new door opens to a world you didn't even know existed."

She stood in silence in front of him, then said, "I'll come back."

Maybe she's right, he thought. *Maybe, instead of feeling defeated, I should think of what I want to happen?*

Ricky glanced over to where Gladys was at the other end of the counter, talking to another customer. She noticed his glance and returned.

"Hi, I'm back. Or would you rather I leave you alone? I don't mean to bother you."

"Oh, no, no. In fact, I think you may have something there."

"Seems to me that we both have a score to settle with Digwood. You know, perhaps we can think of the possibilities together. I serve on the city council. I don't have anything specific in mind, yet, but I believe that there are no coincidences. Maybe this is not the place and time to discuss this."

"Well, if not right now, it soon will be," she replied.

"Here's my phone number." She jotted it down on a cocktail napkin and slid it to him. "If, or when, you're up to discussing the possibilities, call me. We can grab a cup of coffee and talk some more. Speaking of more, would you like another?"

"Oh, no, no, thank you. Now that I think more about it, I'm better off keeping my wits about me. I think I'll settle-up."

"Your tab?"

"Yeah, well, I'll start with my tab. But I think I'll give what you've been saying, some thought. There are other things I will need to settle-up."

"There you go. Get yourself on the agenda instead of the menu! I'll look forward to talking with you further, young man."

The End...
of book two.

PETER SANDEL

Arriving in Central Oregon at age 5, Peter Sandel grew up inspired by the beauty and natural history of the Pacific Northwest. Walking to and from Bear Creek Elementary School, in Bend, he would notice the ground squirrels foraging through the ponderosa pinecones. Examining the cones, he discov-ered pine nuts and began to nibble on them. Finding them to be a tasty treat, he soon became drawn into the environment around him. So much so, that throughout his young life, the Deschutes River Canyon became his most sacred place.

The first scene of the story was inspired by a real experience Peter had at the top of Lava Butte in Central Oregon, where Peter met the first of two of Central Oregon's finest, Phil Brogan, author of "East of the Cascades," and later, near Fort Rock, Rube Long, co-author of "The Oregon Desert." These two men were "living Central Oregon history." Their words made a big impression on Peter Sandel at a very early age.

Peter would spend many a morning along the Deschutes River, breathing in the sweet-spicy air and watching the sun peak over the rimrock, as the creatures of the canyon began their day. These times along the river would become the most formative of his life.

The family would soon move over the mountains to Salem Oregon, where Peter graduated from Sprague High School and then Oregon State University. During summer months, before and during college, he fought forest fires for the Oregon State Department of Forestry.

After college, Peter spent the next 30 years making his living writing, designing and illustrating as an art director and creative director in locations from the San Francisco Bay Area, to Portland Oregon, and Montana. He has developed and produced everything from advertising campaigns, annual reports, and capability brochures, to SEO copy and other online content, winning several awards for this work.

Peter Sandel's tranquil times along the Deschutes River, hiking and fishing with his father and brother, provided him with insights that would influence him for the rest of his life. While sitting for hours among the local inhabitants of the canyon, he began to understand more about each of them, and the interactions between them. These were the stories and images that would inspire him to create the world of RIMROCK.

www.rimrockbooks.com

ALSO BY

RIMROCK

The Illumination Stone

The Cavern of Ahtūn

Book 3—To Be Announced